Rescued By the Captain

Rescued By the Captain

Laura A. Barnes

Laura A. Barnes

2017

First Printing: 2017

ISBN: 9781072713494

Laura A. Barnes

www.lauraabarnes.com

Cover Art by Cheeky Covers

Editor: Polgarus Studios

To: William-for being my inspiration.

To: Ashley, Nicholas, & Joshua

Thank you for all your love and support in helping make my dream

come true.

Chapter One

Somewhere in the North Sea

April 1810

THORN STOOD AT THE bow of his ship, *My Hedera,* and stared into the dark night, lost in deep thought. The brigantine dipped and swayed into the huge waves. Dark storm clouds stretched across the skies and blended into the black sea. None of the stars lit the sky because the heavens had opened for a fierce storm. He ran his fingers through his long, dark, wet hair, and then brought his hands down to his sides, fisting them in anger. The storm was nothing compared to the turmoil of emotions that ran through him.

"Captain, do you think it's her?" His first mate shouted to be heard above the thunder as he twisted his hat in his hands.

"I don't know Sammy. I don't know," Thorn whispered into the storm.

Marcus Thornhill, Thorn, to his friends continued to stare into the dark night. He knew it was her, but he just didn't want to admit to it to himself. As he tried to gain control of his anger, he also tried to figure out who would have done such an awful thing to her. He needed to be calm before his return, but he was furious with himself. If he would have come home sooner, he could have prevented this from happening.

Thorn made his way down the stairs to his cabin, where he found her asleep on his bed. She hadn't woken since they discovered her in the small lifeboat adrift aimlessly in the sea. He didn't know how long she had been out there, but her clothes were soaked through from the rain. The night air was frigid, and she would have frozen to death if they had gotten to her any later. Thorn could still remember how her body felt as he lifted her from the boat—chilled to the bone, lips blue, and body shaking uncontrollably.

He was grateful Sammy had been on the lookout for any suspicious ships in the area and had called Thorn to investigate when he'd spied the lifeboat in the open sea. Thorn didn't know if it was a trap or not, so he decided to row to the boat himself to see what floated in the middle of nowhere.

He was not prepared for what he saw—a lifeless, abandoned girl with nothing for her comfort. He climbed into the boat and knelt next to the girl, pulling her wet hair away from her face. Long and blonde, it clung to her cheeks and neck. His heart stopped as he took in what he saw as a familiar face of his past. It looked like her, but he wasn't sure. He only knew he must get her to safety.

He lifted her from the puddle of water that had collected in the boat. As he lifted her in his arms, he yelled at his men for a blanket. He passed her to one of his men as he made his way back onto the boat. As he settled down, he wrapped her in the blanket and held her tight in his arms.

"Get us back to ship swiftly!" Thorn shouted at his men.

As they rowed back, the rain started again and pelted their bodies harshly. Thorn pulled her closer into the warmth of his body to protect her from the storm.

When they returned to the ship, Thorn ordered someone to take her to his cabin. As Jake carried out his order, Thorn ordered the rest of the crew to prepare the ship for a storm.

He had so many questions that needed answered, but for now he had to help her stay alive. She had to live, because without her, his life wasn't worth living.

She lay on his bed so lifeless. If it weren't for her soft moans, Thorn would have thought she died while he was on the top deck. Thorn reached to touch her red cheek to realize her body burned. He went to the door and called for Sammy.

Sammy limped into the room. "What do you need, Capt'n?"

"Fetch me some wet towels. I need to bring down her fever."

Sammy left the cabin and returned quickly, bringing with him a bowl of cold water and towels. He watched as the captain wetted the towels and gently wiped them over the young girl's face. He noticed how the captain took such gentle care of her, like she was a priceless doll. He had never seen this side of the captain before, not that he was a cold man, but during times of war, the captain couldn't show his softer side. They'd all be dead if he did.

"Capt'n?" Sammy tried to get Thorn's attention.

Thorn turned toward Sammy, realizing Sammy was still in his cabin. He raised his eyebrows at him in silent inquiry of why he still remained.

"The storm is getting worse, sir. We need you on deck," Sammy stuttered.

"Get all hands on deck and steer her to calmer seas yourself. I'm needed here. I cannot abandon her again," Thorn shouted in annoyance.

Sammy left the cabin, climbed on deck, and called all men on deck to help him get the ship to safer waters. Sammy directed the crew to their positions while he took his position behind the wheel. The crew worked to lower the sails while Sammy started to steer them out of the storm. They had their work cut out for them tonight because the wind was strong, and the sea was rougher than ever. Their feet were unsteady on deck as the sea threw the ship back and forth between the waves. *It will be a miracle to keep this boat afloat,* Sammy thought, but he planted his feet firmly and held onto the ship's wheel for dear life.

Chapter Two

SHE MOANED SOFTLY. THORN pulled the covers back and noticed she still wore the sea and rain-soaked dress. When Thorn realized that was the cause for her fever, he slowly cut the wet dress from her body. As he pulled away the soaked material and wiped her dry with a towel. He slid off her chemise, lay her back on the bed, and pulled the covers over her naked body. Her body was on fire and grew hotter by the moment.

Thorn reached for the washcloth and dipped it into the cold water. He slid the wet towel gently over her body and tried to cool her. He repeated this over and over to bring her comfort. As he did this, he noticed the long scar that ran along the back of her thigh. He traced the scar with his finger.

"Ivy," he whispered.

It was her. When he gazed upon her face, he saw the woman he loved. Thorn noted the subtle changes from youth to womanhood that occurred since last he'd last saw her.

His last memory of her was of a young beauty of sixteen on the verge of womanhood, but seven years had passed since then. In those years, she matured into a beautiful temptress. Even wet and sick she was all he desired. He also observed the beads of sweat dotting her forehead as a fever overtook her body. It appeared she grew worse.

She mumbled in her sleep and did not make sense at first. Then as the night wore on, her cries grew louder. Thorn could hear the misery in her voice as she spoke in her sleep.

"You have to help me escape, Tommy. Please, you can come with me."

"Charles, you must go to the authorities with this information."

"I feel so alone, there is no one else to help me. There is one person, but I know he will never return."

Her sickness continued for two days before she took a turn for the worse. It seemed like she gave up the fight to live. She no longer talked and thrashed around. Her body grew hotter and more lifeless. Then the chills overtook her body. Thorn felt so helpless, he didn't know what more he could do for her. He fed her water from a spoon and wiped her body countless times with cold, wet towels. Even as he held her hand and spoke soothing words it didn't help her get any better.

Meanwhile, the boat rocked and groaned as it fought the fierce sea, rising high above the water, floating in midair for a few brief seconds, only to slam back upon the rough waters. It would repeat this over and over throughout the days and nights. Sammy would come in, give him reports, serve him food, and ask about the lass. The crew appeared to hold their own. He trusted Sammy to keep it under control.

On the third day, they hit quieter waters. It still rained, sometimes heavier than others but not as fierce. But she became worse. Thorn slid off his clothes and crawled under the covers with her. He pulled her body against his and gave her all his warmth. She felt so small and lifeless in his arms. As his hands slid along her body, he hoped to warm her up. Her chills shook them both. Thorn heard her teeth rattle together. He spent the night like this as he touched her and whispered words into her ears. Thorn wanted her to know he was there and to fight. Not to give up. He would be here for her when she awoke.

Thorn drifted to sleep this way and held her close to his heart. When he awoke a few hours later he noticed her chills stopped and the fever had come down. He sensed they were almost out of the woods. He did not want to let her go, so he tightened his hold on her and drifted back to sleep.

When Thorn awoke again, he watched her sleep as he held her. He understood this was wrong. She was out of harm's way, and he shouldn't lie with her this way. Even though nothing happened, he had compromised her. Yet, Thorn didn't want to release her from his embrace. This was the only time he could remain with her with his guard relaxed, and he wished for a few more precious moments. Beautiful didn't even begin to describe her. Even in sickness she held the look of an angel. She always was his angel from heaven.

He softly stroked her cheek and touched the softness of her skin against his rough hands. They were callused from all the hard work he performed on his ship. Thorn remembered the last time he touched her cheek—in another time and another place. Seven years ago. So much had happened since then, but he remembered the day like it was yesterday.

He watched her as she picked the flowers in his mother's garden. She was so young, so fresh, and he realized he shouldn't feel for her as he did. There were too many years separating them. But he was in love with her. She was bent over the rose bush as she talked to the flowers about how beautiful they were and how wonderful they would look for his mother in her bedroom. Her eyes rose and noticed him as he watched her.

"Oh, Marcus, you scared me. I didn't see you standing there. Your mother, she is well, isn't she?"

"Yes, she is fine, just resting," Marcus answered.

"Oh good. I have been so worried about her."

"I know you have been. You have been so helpful through her sickness. We are forever grateful to you, My Lady."

"Marcus, don't 'My Lady' me. We are family. You know I think of your mother as mine. Our fathers are best friends, just like you and Charles."

"Are we friends, Ivy?" Marcus asked softly.

Ivy blushed a pretty shade of pink as she lowered her head and sighed. "Yes, Marcus, we are friends."

Marcus wanted to be more than friends with her. He reached out and gently stroked her cheek as he ran his thumb across her lips. She raised her head to stare into his eyes.

"Marcus?" Ivy asked in confusion.

He bent his head to brush his lips across hers, so gently he could barely feel their lips touch. But it was enough for him to feel an impact in his very soul. Ivy gasped and dropped her basket of flowers. She stood on her tiptoes to reach his lips to better press them into his. Thorn groaned and brought her deeper into his arms. He pulled her higher on his chest and devoured her mouth. When she responded with eagerness, he kissed her deeply, a long, slow, gentle kiss to draw out her sweetness, breath by breath.

He could feel Ivy grab onto his shoulders to hang on tightly. He softly brushed his lips against hers as he pulled away. Thorn stared as Ivy slowly opened her eyes. Her eyes were dazed as she stared into his. Then when she became aware of his hold on her, she blushed even deeper.

"Forgive me, Ivy. I shouldn't have done that," Marcus said as he lowered Ivy to her feet and slowly drew away from her. "I have overstepped my bounds, especially because of all that you have done for us these past two weeks."

Ivy looked away and twisted her hands together as she glanced at the flowers. When she realized she dropped them, she bent down to gather them again and remained quiet. Marcus knelt to assist her with the flowers and help her to her feet.

"Say something, Ivy. I am so sorry. I never should have pressed myself onto you."

Ivy stared at him as a tear slid from her eye and whispered, "Why did you?"

"I can't explain it, and you are too young to understand the depth of my feelings for you. I am too old for you. I couldn't help myself when I glimpsed at you standing there. You have been so helpful to us here at Thornhill," Thorn explained as he wiped the tear from her cheek.

"So, you kissed me out of gratitude?" Ivy asked in shock.

"No, the kiss meant nothing in regard to gratitude. You looked so pretty in the garden. With the sun shining down on your hair, you are a breath of fresh air to gaze upon."

Ivy put her fingers to her lips and whispered, "Do you regret kissing me?"

Marcus grabbed Ivy's hands and held them in his. He leaned over and gently placed a kiss on top of her head as he squeezed her hands.

"No, our kiss is one thing in my life I will never regret. But it was a mistake. Nothing can ever come of this."

"Why?" Ivy asked.

"Because we are wrong for each other, and I am leaving tonight. I don't know when I will return or if I will return from this war. Also, you are going to London for your first season. I won't take that opportunity away from you."

"I don't care about the season. I only want you. I've only ever wanted you. I love you, Marcus."

"But I don't love you, Ivy."

Marcus watched as the color left Ivy's face as she gasped. She lifted her hand to her mouth; her fingers touched her lips as she looked into Thorn's eyes. He felt her tears before he saw them slide slowly out of her eyes and trail down her cheeks. She ran into the house, leaving him in the garden to become like all the other statues in his mother's garden when he turned to stone.

Thorn watched her sleep. That was all he had done for five days. His hands shook as he poured whiskey into a glass, the liquid sloshing all over. He raised the glass to his mouth, downed the whiskey, and felt the burn travel into his chest. The whiskey didn't seem to do the trick he wanted it to. He still felt chilled to the bone from the thought that he might lose her before he even got to have her. Thorn poured himself one after another as he continued to watch her for any change.

He realized getting drunk was not the wisest course of action right now. But he didn't see any other way to ease the ache in his heart. Thorn wanted to yell, scream, and pound out his anger. Not that any of that would be fair to his crew or to the young lady who lay helpless in his bed. He would get his revenge one day on whoever was responsible for this.

Chapter Three

WHILE SAMMY BATTLED THE FIERCE storm, Thorn battled the fiercest storm of Ivy's life. The sun broke through the small window at the same moment her fever broke. As the sea settled into gentle waves, he waited for her to awaken, to show more sign of life. He needed to hear her speak his name.

As the soft light of dawn rose and shined in on her, Thorn noticed her lashes flutter softly against her cheek. He rose swiftly from his chair, toppling it to the floor as he rushed to her side. He gently brushed her long, blonde hair back from her face and held his breath to see if she finally awakened.

Her eyelids rose slowly as she came out of her deep sleep. She looked around and took in her surroundings. Thorn could see the confusion in her eyes as she glanced around the cabin before they settled on him.

"Marcus?" she whispered.

Thorn was so overcome with emotion he couldn't answer her. He slid his hand down and laced his fingers through hers. He brought her hand to his mouth and brushed his lips across her fingers.

"My sweet Ivy," he whispered back.

He sat on the edge of the bed and held onto her hand as his eyes roved over her body, making sure she was truly with him again. He felt so relieved. Thorn had feared this moment would never happen.

Ivy tried to sit up, but her body was weak. She fell back onto the pillows and moaned.

"What happened?" she asked Thorn.

Thorn rested next to her on the bed and adjusted the blankets around her body. He softly brushed her hair back from her face to let the softness drift through his fingers. Thorn laid his hand across her forehead to satisfy his curiosity that her fever had broken, and he let out a sigh when he felt her cool skin.

"You have been sick with a fever," he told Ivy.

Ivy stared into Thorn's eyes with confusion and asked, "How?"

"Well that is what I was hoping you would tell me. We found you drifting in a lifeboat in the open sea. How did you come to be there?" Thorn asked.

Ivy closed her eyes, brought her hand to her forehead, and rubbed her temples. Her head and body ached so badly. She really didn't understand how she ended up on the lifeboat. She knew what happened to her before that, but she wasn't ready to discuss it yet, especially with Thorn. He would think her so naïve, like he always did. She opened her eyes and saw how concerned Thorn was for her. Ivy didn't want to, but she lied to him.

"I cannot recall. I'm trying to remember, but I just don't know."

Ivy moaned as she tried to get comfortable. She avoided eye contact with Thorn. He would know she lied because he always knew when she told the truth.

"It is all right, Ivy. Don't worry yourself. We will get the answers in time. The most important thing now is for you to get well."

Thorn laid a wet towel across her forehead.

"Close your eyes and rest. I will get you some broth and fresh water."

Ivy lay back on the bed and closed her eyes while she listened to Thorn move around the cabin as he picked up items and put them away. She peeked out from the cloth and stared as he made his way to the door. He still looked as good as he did seven years ago, even with a full-grown beard and appearing like he hadn't changed his clothes in a week. Ivy watched as Thorn left the cabin.

She slowly slid her body up the bed and started to slide her legs over when it dawned on her that she felt naked underneath the blanket. Ivy glanced under the blanket, and she was, indeed, naked. Her body grew warm as a blush spread over her entire body. Ivy gasped and grabbed the blanket tighter against herself. Where had her clothes gone? Who had taken the clothes off her body? Did Thorn see her naked? She was embarrassed and didn't know how to broach the subject with him. There was no way she could remain unclothed. She needed clothes, and she wanted to freshen up but didn't want Thorn to walk in on her. Ivy was trapped in his bed with nowhere to go but to wait for him to return.

Thorn walked in and noticed Ivy resting on the edge of the bed with a charming blush spread across her cheeks. If he was not mistaken, it also spread across the rest of her body. What he wouldn't do to view that. He imagined the soft red blush coloring her pale, soft skin, the color highlighting her softness into a warm glow. He felt himself harden at the thought of touching her and being entranced into the glow. Thorn realized he needed to get his thoughts under control and see to her comfort. But as he gazed at her all innocent and insecure, it only seemed to strengthen his desire. He closed his eyes for a moment to help him refocus on her comfort. By the time he opened his eyes, he had his mind and body under control.

"I have some broth for you to drink."

"Um, Thorn, where are my clothes?"

"I'm sorry, Ivy, but I had to cut them off you."

"Why?" Ivy asked.

"Because you were soaked through when we found you in the lifeboat. Your clothes were stuck so tightly to you, I had to remove them in a hurry and warm your body. The only way for me to achieve that was to cut them off with my knife," Thorn explained.

Ivy stared at Thorn with her mouth slightly open. She was embarrassed and didn't know how to answer. Thorn had seen her naked. Ivy glanced away, she could never stare him in the eyes again. Not sure how to respond, she lowered her eyes to stare as her fingers nervously picked at the blanket. Her fingers became more agitated as embarrassment overcame her.

Thorn could see how embarrassed Ivy was, so he decided to take pity on her. He went to his chest and dug out a shirt. He took the shirt over to her and laid it across her hands. Ivy gripped the soft fabric of his shirt, and her fingers sank into the softness. Thorn then turned his back to her. As he turned around, Ivy brought the shirt up to her nose and sniffed it. She closed her eyes. It smelled like Thorn, which was like heaven to her senses.

"Do you need any help placing the shirt on your body?"

"No, I can manage on my own," Ivy choked out.

Ivy slipped Thorn's shirt over her head and slid it along her body. It hung to her knees. To wear his shirt felt the same as when his warm arms embraced her all those years ago. She wrapped her arms around herself and stared at Thorn's back. Ivy's eyes roamed over his body as she took in every detail. He still looked as gorgeous as ever. His black hair was longer since the last she had set eyes upon him. It hung past his shoulders, and he kept raking his fingers through it as he waited on her before he could turn around. She noticed how his body had filled out with more muscles. Thorn was always in shape, but he appeared even more dangerous now. The years at war on his ship had shaped his body from the young man of leisure to a grown man with a purpose. He still made her heart beat fast, as it was now, and this was only the backside of him. The front side of Thorn was even more dangerous to gaze upon.

As Ivy's eyes roamed back up his body, she noticed Thorn had looked over his shoulder at her and had seen her admiring him. When Ivy's eyes met his, he turned his head around and cleared his throat.

"Are you finished getting dressed?"

"Yes, Thorn. You can turn around."

Ivy bent her head to straighten the shirt around her knees, not wanting to meet his eyes. She was embarrassed that he'd caught her staring at him. She slid the blanket over her legs for something to keep her distracted. First, he saw her naked, then he caught her as she looked his body over as if she was starved for him.

Thorn watched Ivy and smiled to himself. He wanted to comment on her sightseeing but didn't want to embarrass her any more than she already was. So, he reached for the broth and sat down next to her, extending the cup toward her.

"Drink a little of this, it will help you get stronger."

Ivy reached for the cup, and her hand brushed against his. The touch of his hand was warm against her skin. His fingers lingered against hers as she lifted the cup to her mouth. She sipped the warm broth and felt her insides warm up. Whether it was from the touch of Thorn's hand or the broth she didn't know. She finished the broth and handed the cup back to

Thorn. Ivy tucked her hair behind her ears and slid against the pillows. She brought her hand to her mouth and yawned. Her eyelids lowered, and she tried to open them wider.

"I'm sorry, Thorn. I am so tired."

"Close your eyes. You need to rest."

Thorn watched as Ivy drifted back to sleep. He slid the blankets back over her and tucked her into his bed. He leaned over to softly kiss her forehead. As he watched her sleep, he thought how grateful he was that she would be well. With enough rest, she would be back too normal soon, and then they could find the answers they needed.

Thorn knew she lied to him earlier. She might not have known how she came to be on the lifeboat, but she knew more than she let on. Why would she keep it a secret from him? Didn't she understand he would do anything for her? He realized she thought he didn't care, but that was far from the truth.

He knew Charles and Ivy were in trouble somehow. He would find out why and fix it for them, no matter what it took. Charles was his best friend and was like a brother to him. They had been involved in many jams together and always helped each other. It had to have something to do with the mysterious letter he sent Thorn a few months ago. Charles asked for help and he ignored it because it involved Ivy. It wasn't that he didn't want to see Ivy. He did. He just didn't know how much longer he could go on in life pretending she didn't exist. Even though he hadn't seen her in seven years, his love for her only grew stronger. He didn't think it was possible, but when he pulled her from the lifeboat, the feelings he had for her knocked him over. The anger and grief he experienced at that moment overwhelmed him. His emotions were still overpowering as he remembered her pale, lifeless body as it lay in a puddle of water at the bottom of the boat. Who did this to her and why?

These were questions Ivy would answer as soon as she recovered. He needed to regain her trust. He understood that he'd hurt her years ago, and he had to do everything in his power to make it up to her. He remembered she was once in love with him, but the question he needed answered the most was if she still loved him today and would she love him forever? It was left to him to show her how much he loved her and that he would love her forever.

Chapter Four

WHEN IVY AWOKE, SHE realized she was alone in the cabin. She slowly slid from the bed, and her body shook as she tried to stand. She walked alongside the bed and held onto the edges until she was steady on her feet. Ivy released her hold and shuffled to the desk, her balance off as the ship swayed up and down with the waves. She clutched the desk, and as she slid into the chair her legs buckled underneath her. Her hands shook as she ran the tips of her fingers across the desk. When she closed her eyes, she pictured Thorn sitting there, plotting over his maps for the best course to direct his ship.

She knew Thorn worked for the government during the war and that they still sent him on special missions. She'd overheard their fathers discussing him late one night, and Ivy understood why he left her the way he did. They hadn't realized she listened to their conversations about his dangerous missions. Everybody tried to keep it a secret from her. They thought she was too young and wouldn't understand. To keep her distracted, her father had pushed her into the London seasons over the years and attempted to marry her off countless times. But Ivy had wanted nobody but Thorn, and she would wait for him, even if it took forever. His mother was the only one who understood. Ivy never told her about the kiss, but

Katherine seemed to understand something had happened between them before he left.

Ivy rested her fingers against her lips and sighed softly. She could still feel the touch of his lips against hers after all these years. She also remembered the way he held her in his arms and whispered her name. Ivy never shared that passion with anybody but Thorn. She had never wanted to. Numerous gentlemen courted her, but nobody could make her feel the way Thorn made her feel. To savor his lips against hers again would be magical. But she must stay strong. She couldn't let him hurt her again. These last few years without him had been lonely, and she didn't want to live that way again.

There was a knock on the cabin door, and Ivy bid them to enter. A servant walked in and carried a tray of food.

"Well, lass, don't you look like a beautiful summer flower. It is so good to see you up and about. I've brought you something to eat."

"Thank you, sir. What is your name?" Ivy asked.

"My name is Samuel, but everybody calls me Sammy," he answered as he took off his hat and bowed.

Ivy smiled. "Well Sammy, thank you for the food. Do you know where Thorn is?"

"Well, miss, the captain is tending to ship's business. He said to let you know he will be in later to check in on you and that I am to get you whatever you need in the meantime."

"I only need fresh water to clean with."

Sammy laid the tray of food on the desk, talking to her as he moved the plates to the desk.

"You get eatin' this. The captain wants you stronger."

As Ivy sat and ate the plates of bread and cheese, Sammy went to fetch her fresh water. He limped in with the water and started to clean the cabin.

"I've never seen the captain so happy since you woke up, lass. He was might worried about you. Took care of you all by himself and wouldn't let me help him at all. Gave me the task of steering the ship to safer waters. Don't know who had the tougher job." Sammy laughed.

Ivy smiled as she listened to Sammy talk about Thorn.

"How did you get hurt, Sammy? Did you slip on deck during the storm? I see you are limping."

"Oh no, miss, that's just an old injury acting up. Got that limp a few years back. If it weren't for the captain I would have been a whole lot worse off. It acts up in the rain, it does."

"What happened?"

"The captain saved my life that is what happened. I'm in his debt, lass. Not a better man around. You see it was like this ..."

"That's enough, Sammy," Thorn spoke from the door.

Thorn stopped Sammy before he told Ivy how he saved his life. He didn't need Ivy to believe him to be a hero. While he was the one who saved Sammy's life, he was also the one who risked Sammy's life too. His first mate had the story all wrong, for Thorn was in the sailor's debt, not the other way around.

"Yes, Captain," Sammy mumbled as he walked out the door. "Just trying to sing your praises. Guess I won't make that mistake again."

Thorn smiled as he closed the door to the cabin. He leaned against it as he stared across the cabin at Ivy curled in his chair at the desk. She looked so much healthier. Her face wasn't as pale anymore and her eyes looked refreshed as she gazed back at him. Thorn crossed his arms across his chest.

"Well you are looking refreshed," Thorn commented.

"I hope you don't mind me sitting at your desk?" Ivy asked as she ran her fingers across its top.

Thorn watched her fingers slid back and forth across the grain of the desk. As he watched how her fingers slid over the grooves, he imagined her fingers sliding over the grooves of his body. Her soft fingers would dip and sway along his arms and chest, his whole entire body marked as she marked the desk with her touch now.

"You are welcome anywhere on this ship, Ivy. How are you feeling?"

"I am still a little tired, but my body was stiff lying in bed. I wanted to move around and ended up here."

Ivy noticed Thorn didn't look at her but watched her fingers move across the desk. She stopped her fingers and slid her hands into her lap. Thorn looked up quickly. He cleared his throat as he moved away from the door and came to sit on the corner of the desk.

"Are you ready to talk about your ordeal?" Thorn asked.

"Aren't you needed on deck? I realize I have kept you from your duties. Sammy told me how much work you need to do."

Ivy tried to distract Thorn. She needed time to think and put her thoughts in order. Also, she needed to stall Thorn from all the questions he wanted answered.

Thorn saw the panic in Ivy's eyes. She was scared and hiding something. He didn't want to frighten her, so he decided to give her time to work out her thoughts. He stepped back from the desk and walked over to his chest and dug around for a coat to wear. Sammy steered them off course during the storm, so it would be a few days before they could dock the ship. He had plenty of time to earn her trust. After he shrugged on his coat, he turned toward Ivy.

"Yes, my lady, I am needed elsewhere for the moment. If you would excuse me, I must attend to the duties of my ship. If you have need of anything, Sammy is at your disposal." Thorn walked toward Ivy and bent over to place a kiss on her head.

"I am so relieved you are alive and well." He turned and strode from the cabin.

Ivy remembered the last time Thorn placed a kiss on her forehead like it was yesterday.

She had been in the garden where she gathered flowers for Thorn's mother, Katherine. Ivy had stayed at Thornhill Manor for two weeks as she took care of Thorn's mother, who was ill. Katherine was the mother Ivy never had after her own mother passed away when she was five. She had practically grown up at Thornhill. Their fathers were best friends and so were Ivy's brother, Charles, and Thorn. The boys were inseparable, sometimes for good, but mostly they were caught in trouble. Ivy always tried to tag along after them, but the six year age difference sometimes made it too difficult to keep up with them. During those times, she and Katherine spent time together. So, when she became ill, Ivy rushed to Thornhill to care for her.

That was where Thorn found her on that glorious summer day, as she picked flowers. As she talked to the flowers, she heard the soft crunch of somebody as they walked on the gravel behind her. She turned and noticed Thorn leaned against one of the statues in the garden as he watched her. Ivy remembered blushing when she saw him. Thorn always flustered Ivy when she was near him. She didn't understand why she got so tongue-tied, why her palms would sweat, and why she always seemed to wear a permanent blush around him. Not to mention why if felt like her heart would beat right out of her chest.

Ivy had always loved Thorn, but her feelings for him changed over that year. Like the moments when a spark ignited in their touch as their fingers brushed against each other. When their eyes would meet and they would have their own unspoken conversation. The connection seemed to have grown stronger, and there were times when she had seen the same longing in Thorn's eyes when he watched her.

Ivy didn't recall the exact words that were spoken, but she was in awe of Thorn's flirtation with her. Thorn had never flirted with her, always just treating her like a kid sister. He always trifled with the sophisticated women of the aristocracy and the maidens in the village, but never with her.

She thought to when Thorn ran his thumb across her lip and pulled her into his arms and gently kissed her. His kiss was so soft against her lips. Ivy remembered she slid her hands around his neck and ran her fingers through his hair. As she stood on her tiptoes, she brought his mouth to her lips to deepen the kiss. She could feel the slide of his tongue across her lips as it guided her mouth to open for him. His tongue slid inside her mouth softly, stroking against her tongue. Touching her. Tasting her.

Ivy moaned into his mouth. He'd lifted her higher against his body and pressed her breasts against his chest. Ivy clung to his shoulders, light-headed as he devoured her mouth.

Ivy had never been kissed before and had dreamed of this moment forever. To have his arms embrace her and his lips against hers had felt so wonderful. Ivy also recalled the loss as he pulled away from her to set her away from him. He told her how wrong it was that he kissed her and asked for her forgiveness. She could still remember what a fool she had been, confessing her love for him and begging him to love her in return. But worst of all was her memory of his rejection as he told her he didn't return her love.

At Thorn's desk, Ivy reached and slid her fingers though her hair where he had placed his lips again and kissed her, as he had kissed her all those years ago. She still loved him and always would, but this time it would be different. She would not let him know of her love. She would guard her heart. And to guard her heart, she also had to guard her secrets.

Chapter Five

THORN STAYED AWAY FROM the cabin all day and didn't return until late in the night. He stayed away on purpose to give Ivy her space. He didn't want to pressure her because he needed to rebuild the trust they had long ago. And to do that, he knew he had to stay away. Just being near her made him want to protect her and take care of her problems. But he could tell by the look in her eyes when she lied to him that she didn't want to trust him with her troubles. So, he figured if he gave her time to be comfortable in his presence again, it would make her want to confide in him.

As Thorn came into the cabin, he noticed Ivy was curled asleep in his chair, her long legs tucked beneath his white linen shirt. Her head was tilted off to the side, which looked uncomfortable. Thorn bent over and lifted her into his arms. Ivy moaned as she settled her head underneath his chin. She snuggled into his arms and rested her hand in the opening of his shirt. Thorn stilled as Ivy's fingers touched his skin. He closed his eyes at her innocent caress. His need for her overwhelmed him, and he could only imagined how he would react if she touched his body out of her need for him. Thorn pulled her closer to his chest as he walked over to the bed and held her for a few moments, gazing upon her sleeping face.

He didn't want to lie her down; she was unguarded like this. It was as if he regarded the old Ivy, the one who trusted him and told him everything. He didn't understand how to feel or act with the new Ivy, the one who kept secrets from him, who looked at him with guarded eyes full of mistrust and hurt. The hurt in her eyes pierced his soul more than anything. He would do whatever it took to wipe that stare away. He would persuade her to look at him again with trust and happiness, but most of all with love.

He lay her gently on the bed and tucked the blankets around her so she wouldn't catch a chill. As he stood, he felt weary. He decided he would lie down for a few moments on top of the covers to think of his next course of action. Exhaustion overtook his body as he sunk into the bed, tired from the care he had given her the last few days and from the problems with the ship. The ship needed minor repairs from the storm, and they had gone farther out to sea than Thorn wanted. They were off course. But before they arrived into port, he needed time to convince Ivy to trust him and to confide how she became lost at sea. Thorn closed his eyes and drifted to sleep.

Ivy awoke to find herself wrapped in Thorn's arms. She raised her eyes to his face to see he was still deep asleep. He looked much younger in his sleep, as his hair fell over his forehead and his face relaxed in slumber. Ivy realized how tired he must have been between the care of his ship and from his attention as he nursed her from her illness. She saw the weariness in him yesterday and realized she didn't help him by holding onto her secrets. Ivy felt safe here in his arms and she closed her eyes as she savored the contentment.

"Ivy," Thorn moaned in his sleep.

Ivy opened her eyes but saw he still slept. She reached out and softly ran her fingers across his forehead to brush his hair from his eyes. Ivy continued to run her fingers across his eyebrows and down his cheeks. She could stare at him like this all day. Unguarded. Ivy watched as Thorn slowly slid his eyes open to look deep into her eyes. The warmth of his dark blue eyes seemed to touch deep into Ivy's soul and heated her up. He tightened his arms around her and pulled her body closer into his.

He gently placed his lips against hers to kiss her fully awake. Ivy weakened by the softness of his kiss to her lips. She moaned as she slid her fingers through his long, dark hair. Thorn growled as his kiss deepened. He slid his tongue across her lips to place soft kisses against them. Ivy opened her mouth and Thorn slid his tongue inside Ivy's mouth to slowly stroke her fires. When Ivy touched her tongue to Thorn's tongue it made him kiss her more deeply and passionately. Then he stroked his tongue against hers and tasted her fully. Ivy drew his head toward her as she returned his kiss, stroke for stroke. She wanted to taste Thorn just as deeply.

Thorn sensed Ivy's passion for him but knew he couldn't move this fast. She was innocent and did not understand the consequences of this kind of passion. How out of control it could burn until it consumed them. He slowly ended the kiss as he dragged his lips away. He then kissed his way along her neck and murmured her name as he placed little kisses along the way. As he rested his head on her shoulder, he caught his breath and brought his body under control. He felt her heart pound against his chest and realized their kiss affected Ivy to the same degree as it did him.

It took all his willpower to stop when he did. To awake with her in his arms as she watched him and touched him gave him the hope he needed. She still cared for him, and it was all he needed to know. When Ivy tried to pull away, he tightened his hold on her. As he looked into her eyes, he recognized that she'd emotionally pulled away too.

"Good morning, sweet Ivy," Thorn said.

Thorn watched as Ivy blushed her beautiful shade of a red rose when he spoke to her. He laughed and kissed her on the lips, a gentle peck of playfulness. Thorn would never grow tired of her blushes.

She pushed against his chest again and tried to get out of his arms. Ivy was embarrassed to be caught like a wanton hussy as she touched him. What must he think of her? She always seemed to throw herself at him. How desperate did that make her? He only needed to look or touch her, and she melted inside as she turned to mush around him. So, when he kissed her, she wanted more. She needed to get herself under control around him. She must resist his charm and, most of all, his kisses. When Thorn kissed her, she lost all her thoughts, which made her vulnerable. She needed to keep her secrets for a while longer, and if he continued to kiss her like that, she would tell him everything. But then that was probably his plan all along.

Why else would he have stopped with his kisses just now? He already made it clear in the past he didn't love her like that. So, it must be part of his plan to get her to talk, to sweeten her with kisses. Well it would not work on her.

"Good morning, Thorn. You can release me now."

"No, I think I would like to stay this way all day," he teased her.

Thorn wouldn't think it was possible, but Ivy turned an even darker shade of red. He laughed to himself as he thought he should take pity and release her. She pulled away, tugged the blanket tighter around her body, and looked everywhere but at him.

"I am sorry, my dear. I only meant to rest last night and didn't mean to fall asleep lying next to you. Not that I regret it any, my darling. Waking with you in my arms was a dream come true. Nor am I going to ask your forgiveness for our kiss because that was another dream come true for me."

Ivy didn't know what to say. She couldn't tell if he teased her or if he meant what he said, so she stayed quiet. There he went again and confused her with all those "my dears" and "darlings." Another part of his strategy to charm her with his sweet words. Those words probably worked on the other women in his life, but she knew him. She had known him all her life and had seen how he charmed people whenever he wanted something—or someone.

As he smiled to himself, Thorn could tell he confused her. So, he didn't elaborate and left her guessing. He watched as she slid her hair behind her ears, an action she did when she was nervous.

"I will find Sammy, so he can serve us breakfast. I shall return shortly, allowing you a few minutes to refresh yourself."

When Thorn left, Ivy glanced to the side of the bed where he slept. She reached over and ran her hand over the pillow where his head rested, then over her own body. Ivy still savored the warmth of his body—on the pillow and on her. She closed her eyes to relive the moment. Even though it just happened, she still felt herself pressed against him. She didn't know how to react to this Thorn. He was playful. Their last encounter before he left was so serious. This Thorn was the one from childhood, the boy who would always tease her until she blushed. This was the Thorn she'd first fallen in love with.

Chapter Six

THORN MADE HIS WAY to the galley to find Sammy. He found him arguing with Anton, the cook. The two crewmen always bickered at each other's throats. Both thought they knew how he liked his meals better than the other did. Thorn leaned against the wall, smiling, as he regarded their screaming match. There was nothing more fun than watching a French cook and a Scottish sailor disagree.

"You need to get out of my kitchen you Scottish sea urchin," Anton yelled as he pointed his knife at Sammy.

"I wouldn't be here if you weren't trying to send such sissy food off to the captain to eat. He needs food with stamina. Not these girly pastries," Sammy argued back.

"Those are for the mademoiselle, not the captain, you guppy."

Sammy picked up a knife at the insults, thrashing it through the air. As he walked toward the cook, Anton backed away and hit his backside against the counter. Sammy held the knife pointed at his chest.

"You call me one more sea animal name, I will gut you. Do I make myself clear, Frenchie?"

Thorn watched as Anton opened his mouth to argue, but no words came out. He gulped a breath of air, where he looked like a sea animal himself, his face turning bright red in anger. Thorn took pity on Anton and cleared his throat to get their attention.

Sammy dropped the knife on the counter, and Anton busied his hands on preparing a tray. They both understood how much the captain despised any fighting on his ship.

"Ah, Captain, I was just bringing you and the lass something to eat," Sammy said.

"I made the mademoiselle something light to eat. I hope she enjoys, Captain," Anton said, trying to butter up Thorn.

"She will love what you made, Anton, and so will I," Thorn said as he gave Sammy a look that told him to behave.

Thorn followed Sammy out of the galley as they made their way back to his cabin.

"Why do you antagonize him like that? We will have a mutiny on our hands if he jumps ship at the next port. The crew wasn't too happy the last time Anton decided to leave. I have enough on my hands without taking care of your petty squabbles with each other," Thorn said.

Sammy lowered his head as he walked down the passageway, mumbling, "Yes, sir. I'm sorry, sir."

Thorn laughed and slapped him on the back.

"Chin up, old man, let's get the lady fed. I am hoping to get some of my questions answered this morning if I can. Let's see if Anton's cooking will sweeten her up."

Thorn pushed open the door for Sammy and followed him into the cabin. He noticed Ivy had risen from bed. He searched the cabin and found her looking out the porthole window

"Sorry there is not a good view. When you are feeling stronger, you can take a stroll around the deck," Thorn told Ivy.

Ivy turned as Thorn walked deeper into the cabin. She looked past him and saw Sammy come in and set a tray on the desk. Someone filled the tray with a remarkable variety of delicious-smelling pastries. Pastries were Ivy's downfall. She could never eat just one. Everybody knew if they wanted her help with something or to get her to tell a secret all they had to do was bring fresh pastries for her to devour. She would agree to anything and divulge any secret that needed to be whispered. So that was how he would attempt to reach through her defenses. Well, she would enjoy the pastries but stay strong to keep her secrets from him. Did he think she was the same weak girl he left all those years ago?

"Good morning, Sammy. Thank you for breakfast, it looks delicious. You shouldn't have gone too so much trouble."

"Ah, it was no problem, lass. It is my pleasure. How are you feeling?"

"I feel a lot better. Thank you for asking."

"Well enjoy your breakfast, and I will be back later with lunch," Sammy told Ivy.

"When you have time, Captain, there is a matter I need to discuss with you on deck," he told Thorn.

"I will meet you on deck shortly."

Sammy left the cabin. Thorn watched Ivy as she wandered over to the tray and picked a small pastry with an apple on top. He continued to stare as she slid the pastry between her lips and chewed slowly. She licked her lips and softly moaned.

All Thorn could think about was her tongue as it slid across his lips. She did not understand how her innocent acts drove him to distraction. From the way she ate a pastry to the way her hands caressed the desk made Thorn think of her lips as they licked his as her hands caressed him. He needed to get his thoughts under control and focus on how he needed to persuade Ivy to confide in him all her troubles.

He spent too many years away from her. During those times, he missed watching her enjoy the simplest of things, like eating pastries. He knew they were her downfall, which was why he asked Anton to whip up a batch for her this morning. He knew all her weaknesses and strengths, and he wasn't above trying to bribe secrets from her. There were many times he used pastries to get her to talk, like whenever she would hold a clue to the games Charles and he played on each other.

"These are delicious, Thorn. Tell Sammy thank you for me."

"Sammy is not the man to thank. I will let the cook know you loved them. Anton will be pleased. You almost didn't receive any," Thorn told Ivy.

"Why not?"

"They were in a fierce battle over breakfast when I went to the galley."

"What kind of fierce battle?"

"On whether this breakfast here would sustain me, but Anton was only worried whether you would enjoy them. I guess I am no longer important here. My cook only wishes to please you, madam." Thorn bowed.

Ivy laughed as she bit into another pastry. Her tongue darted out to lick off the icing drizzled across the top.

"Do you want any of these? If not, I will eat them all myself."

Thorn watched the enjoyment on her face and saw how relaxed she became in his company again. This was what he wished for and hoped the pastries would accomplish. This was the old Ivy, the one who laughed in his company out of innocent pleasure.

"No, my dear, they are all for you. I remember how you love your sweets. I wouldn't dream of coming between you and them."

Ivy laughed as Thorn teased her. She continued to savor the sweets and left one for Thorn to eat—an act she did when she was younger. Thorn would bring her sweets to sweeten her up; then Ivy would always leave one for him to eat. It was a way to keep him in her company longer. He would bring her treats to coax her to tell him Charles's secrets in their little games, so she would always have Thorn to herself during these times. She wouldn't have to share him with anybody else. During these moments, he would also talk with her about his dreams. Since she wanted to be part of his dreams, she would imagine herself in them as he told them to her. But that's all they ever would be—dreams never to be a part of.

"I've left you one, Thorn."

Thorn reached down, grabbed the pastry, and slid it into his mouth. He softly moaned with delight at the wonderful taste as he drew a chuckle from Ivy.

"Thank you for sacrificing your last sweet for me," Thorn said, teasing Ivy.

Ivy smiled as she poured them tea. She curled back into his chair as she sipped the warm brew. Thorn could never sit in the chair again without images of her curled up in it. She had only done it a handful of times in the last few days, but it seemed like she had done it for years. This whole cabin had her presence in it now, like she had sailed with him for the last seven years, not seven days.

Thorn walked over to the desk and lowered himself to her level. Ivy sat straighter and rested the cup on the desk. She brought her hands to her lap and clasped them tightly. Thorn reached over and covered her hands and gently enfolded them. He saw the expression on her face change from nervous and scared to pleasure back to being nervous and scared again.

"Ivy, we need to talk. I need you to trust me enough to tell me what happened. Whatever it is, we can work through it together."

Ivy realized this moment would come. She'd run out of time. But it was difficult to think when he touched her. Even this innocent touch of his hand over hers made her heart beat faster. She lost her concentration. She needed to think of something to pacify him for a little longer. At least until they returned to shore. Then she could figure out something—except she had no clue what she would do then.

"I've been trying to remember, Thorn, but my mind remains blank," Ivy lied to him.

"How did you come to be on a lifeboat with nothing but the clothes on your body? You can't remember why you were floating out in the middle of nowhere?" Thorn asked.

Ivy pulled away from Thorn, rose from the chair, and walked to the other side of the cabin. She rubbed her head as she paced back and forth. The cabin made even smaller with his presence. She couldn't escape him. She knew he wanted answers, but she had to protect Charles as much as she could and for as long as she could. He wouldn't understand the desperate measures they were in. But at the same time, she needed Thorn's protection.

Thorn watched as Ivy paced back and forth across his cabin. He knew she lied again, but he also watched her struggle. She wanted to tell him, but she protected herself. He wished she would confide in him and tell him her secrets. He needed to persuade her somehow.

"Ivy, let me help you," Thorn pleaded.

Ivy shook her head at him. She did not trust herself to speak. Her eyes pleaded with him to give her time.

He could feel the sorrow in her eyes down to his soul. He wanted to remove the confusion and soothe away her fears. But she needed to trust him. Thorn reached to grab his cap and stuff it on his head. He slid his hands through his coat and stalked to the door. When he turned around, he pierced her with his dark eyes.

"You're running out of time, Ivy," Thorn said as he walked out of the cabin and slammed the door behind him.

He walked to the deck in search of Sammy. Thorn found him as he looked through the scope into the distance. He searched in the same direction and spotted a speck on the horizon. He knew it was a ship, and it was only a matter of time before they had company. It looked like Ivy's admirers were on the lookout for her.

"Is that what you needed to discuss, Sammy?" Thorn asked, nodding his chin toward the speck in the distance.

He held out his hand for the scope. Sammy handed it over, and Thorn looked to see who they would have for company. The ship was unmarked, no friendly flags flying at its staff. An unmarked ship during war meant only one thing. Pirates. He had a hunch on who this particular pirate was. When their ship caught *My Hedera*, he must make sure Ivy stayed hidden. If not, she would be in more danger than she already was.

"Yeah, Captain, it looks like trouble. Do you think that is the ship Lady Ivy came from?"

"I am afraid so Sammy."

"Has she told you anything yet?"

"No, but it looks like she has run out of time. She must talk now."

"What should we do, Captain?"

Thorn looked through the scope to survey their surroundings. He spotted a stretch of land in the distance where they could maneuver the ship into hiding. He only hoped they had enough time to reach it. With a couple of their sails torn from the storm and repairs still being done, it was a long shot. But they must try.

"See that piece of land Sammy?" Thorn pointed into the distance.

"Yes, sir. You want us to steer her there?"

"I think it will be a good hiding place, if we can arrive there before they catch us. Have the crew raise the sails that work and guide her there before dark. While you do that, I'm going below to get my answers."

Thorn turned and marched to his cabin as he heard Sammy give out the shout for all hands on deck. It would take the whole crew to race the ship ahead and hide before the other ship gained more ground on them. He ran down the stairs and threw open the door to the cabin, slamming it against the wall. He needed answers, and answers he would get.

But he received a shock instead; he paused in the doorway stunned by the sight before him. Then he smiled, entered the room, and quietly closed the door behind him. He leaned against the panel with his arms crossed. His eyes slowly devoured the sight before him.

Chapter Seven

IVY LISTENED TO THE SHOUTS above the cabin as the crew hurried to move the ship to a new location. She thought it would be a perfect time to freshen her body. Ivy figured Thorn would be too busy with the crew and his ship. She figured wrong. As she was sliding off Thorn's shirt and cleaning her body with fresh water and soap, the door flung open and startled her.

Ivy stood in shock as she saw Thorn standing in the doorway with a growl on his face. Then she watched as he silently shut the door and leaned against it, as a devilish smile covered his face. She didn't know whether she would rather deal with his growl or the smile. Either way, she was in danger and needed to cover herself. She reached for the towel and covered her body.

Thorn stood there, smiling, and watched her become flustered. He had her right where he wanted her now. One way or another, he would get his answers. First, he would make her his. This afternoon would be productive after all. He didn't speak; he waited for her to talk. His silence would be his weapon.

Ivy was speechless. His silence was unnerving. After she wrapped the towel around her body, she needed to make her way to the bed for the blanket or the fresh shirt she'd laid out. But as soon as she moved to the bed,

Thorn advanced toward her. He'd caught her and would not show mercy on her anymore. He would receive the answers to his questions, and Ivy would be powerless against him. She understood deep in her heart that she would be unable to resist whatever he asked of her—or wanted.

"Thorn, please give me a few moments to get dressed," Ivy stammered.

Thorn shook his head, for he still did not speak to her. He didn't have to; his eyes said it all. They had grown darker with what Ivy could only see as desire. This was the same look he gave her all those years ago in the garden when he had kissed her. His eyes were making love to her as they slowly slid up and down her body taking in every inch of her. Ivy knew she should have been embarrassed to stand naked before him with only a towel to cover herself, but the need in his eyes made her feel desirable. She didn't know how to react. Her body grew warm as he continued to stare at her.

Ivy inched her way over to the bed to grab his shirt to cover her body, but Thorn ripped it out of her hands. He pulled her body against his and slid his arm tight around her waist, trapping her in his hold. He slid his other hand through her hair, loose around her shoulders as his mouth lowered to hers. Thorn held her head as he devoured her lips, staking his claim. He teased his tongue across her lips to slide into her mouth. He heard her whimper, but he couldn't stop himself from tasting her. Thorn kissed her hungrily to let her understand his need for her. She opened her mouth under his, letting him explore her sweet taste. Her body softening against his.

When he pulled away from her lips, he stared into her eyes and saw hers blaze with anger. She began to beat her fists against his chest. It seemed she would fight this attraction that had built between them.

"Why are you being a bully, Thorn? That was uncalled for," Ivy shouted at him.

Thorn didn't release his hold of Ivy. He pulled her even tighter against his body. He felt her naked breasts as they pressed into his chest. He raised his hand to touch her soft skin and ran it along her side. His hand lingered near her breast as his thumb traced the edge. Thorn rubbed little circles closer to her nipples and felt them tighten against his chest. He realized she wanted him too.

"Your time is up, Ivy. I will have my answers now," Thorn demanded.

"I have no answers to give you, Thorn." Ivy continued to lie to him.

"Are you sure about that? Maybe I will have to coax them out of you."

"Let go of me."

Ivy struggled against Thorn and tried to wiggle out of his hold.

Thorn laughed softly. "You aren't going anywhere, my darling Ivy. I guess coaxing it shall be."

Ivy attempted to free herself out of Thorn's arms. She knew it was useless, but she still tried. What did he mean by coaxing it out of her? How would he coax it out of her? She put her hands to his chest to push herself out of his arms, and her fingers touched his bare chest. Without realizing what she did, she let her fingers explore his hard chest where his shirt opened. When her fingers dipped lower into his shirt, she heard Thorn growl. Startled, Ivy pulled her hand out of his shirt and gazed into Thorn's eyes. What she saw both scared and excited her.

His eyes were so intense; she had never seen them so dark before. He looked at her as if he desired her more than anything else. But how could that be? He stated he didn't love her all those years go. But now his eyes spoke something altogether different. Then Ivy realized he didn't have to love her to desire her. How naïve she was. Was his desire and not his love enough for her? Could she let Thorn make love to her without his love?

The only thing Ivy understood was she had been lonely these past seven years without Thorn. His absence left a void she was unable to fill. If making love was the only way to have Thorn, then she needed him to make love to her. She loved him enough for the both of them. This time, she wouldn't tell him. She would be sophisticated like the older women of the ton. She would give him her body but not her heart.

Thorn always could read Ivy by the expression in her eyes. He knew the exact moment when she would be his. As he watched the emotions play through her eyes, he saw the confusion and her need for him. Then he recognized when she decided to open her heart to him. Her eyes took on a soft glow as her body relaxed against his. She decided not to fight what was meant to be. He nibbled his way to her throat, kissing her soft skin. He breathed in her sweet scent and kissed his way back to her ear.

Thorn whispered, "While I loved you wearing my shirt, you look even better in my towel." He watched her blush all over as he slid the towel away from her body. "But you look even more beautiful without the towel."

He bent over and picked her up. She encircled her arms around his shoulders as she pulled his head down for a kiss. She placed her lips against his, kissing him with soft, sweet innocent kisses. As he lowered her body onto his bed, he opened his mouth, inviting her tongue to enter. He let her kiss him as her tongue explored his mouth, tasting him. But his control would only last for so long. Her innocent touch and kisses were pushing him to his limits. He needed to take this slow for her. It was her first time, and he wanted it to be everything she ever dreamed of. He had craved this for years, and his control was on the verge of letting loose; but he must rein in his hunger just a little longer.

Thorn took over the kiss with all the passion he had held back since she awoke a few days earlier. His mouth devoured hers, as his hands stroked along her body. He touched her everywhere, everywhere he had dreamed of for years and was now making it a reality.

"Touch me, Ivy," Thorn whispered.

Ivy glanced into Thorn's eyes and saw his need. She reached to slide her hands down his chest until she reached the buttons on his shirt. She looked back at him again, and he nodded his head at her unanswered question. Ivy's hand shook as she began to unbutton his shirt. She fumbled with the first couple of buttons. Thorn soon lost patience and swept the shirt over his head.

Ivy watched as Thorn removed his shirt, and then ran her hands up the muscles of his arms, feeling their strength ripple under her fingertips. She brought her hands over his shoulders and slid them along his chest. Her fingertips caressed his hard, firm chest and glided down to his stomach. Thorn sucked in a breath as her hands slid lower to brush back and forth across his stomach. She dreamed of this for years, of being able to touch him like this—although nothing had prepared her for this sensation. The feel of his body under her hands made her feel alive and powerful.

Thorn pressed the lower part of his body into Ivy's center. Ivy felt his hardness press into her stomach. It didn't even frighten her; she had waited a lifetime for him.

Ivy softly brushed her hand against the outside of Thorn's pants. She heard Thorn hiss. He suddenly reached down and pulled Ivy's hands into his. He knew he couldn't hold on to his control if she continued touching him there. Thorn already felt like he could explode. Her innocent touch made him slip deeper into a need to release himself into her beautiful body.

Thorn was in heaven. He thought she would be too shy to touch him. His body was on fire. Every stroke of her hand on him only made him hotter. When she brushed her hand against his cock, it took all he could do to stop himself from pulling her legs apart and entering her in one long, slow thrust.

"We need to slow down," Thorn said as he brushed her fingers across his lips.

"Why?" Ivy asked, pressing herself into his hardness.

Ivy placed her lips against his neck to kiss her way to his ear.

"Touch me, Marcus," Ivy whispered.

Marcus moaned from hearing her saying his God-given name, and he kissed Ivy with such passion as his hands slid to her breasts, palming them in his hands. He ran his thumb across her nipples, brushing them back and forth until they hardened like little pebbles. He softly pinched them between his fingers as Ivy moaned into his mouth.

When he slid his mouth away from Ivy's lips, he made his way to her breasts. His tongue slowly circled a nipple and licked softly. He heard Ivy gasp. His tongue licked the tip of her nipple as he sucked it between his lips. It hardened even tighter in his mouth.

Ivy reached to grab Marcus's shoulders as he made love to her breasts. He nibbled on the nipples back and forth, sucking them, kissing them. She ran her fingers through his long dark hair, holding his head to her breasts. The touch of Marcus's lips made Ivy burn. She was hot, and her body felt out of her control. Ivy didn't want him to stop; she wanted more. She didn't know what she wanted, only that she needed more of his touch.

Marcus needed more from her too. He bit on her nipples softly as his hand roamed past her stomach to explore in her curls. She bucked against him as she tried to close her legs.

Marcus pulled his mouth away from her breasts and whispered, "Open for me, Ivy. Please darling. I am only going to help you. You ache there, don't you?"

Ivy nodded her head, too overwhelmed with the sensations coursing through her body. How did he know she ached there, and how could he help her? Ivy slid her legs apart for Marcus, trusting him with her body.

Marcus slid his hand along Ivy's thigh slowly. He brushed his thumb across her clit and touched her heat. He opened her legs wider, sliding his finger up and down across her center. Her wetness soaked his finger, and he moaned as he sucked on her breast again. As he drew her nipple deeper into his mouth, he slid his finger inside her, sinking deep into her wetness. He felt Ivy press herself into his finger, and he moaned. Going so slowly was driving him senseless, but it was so pleasurable. He had never in his lifetime experienced this kind of connection with another woman before. But Marcus knew it would be like this with her.

He slid his finger in and out of Ivy, building up her pressure. As his fingers were pleasuring her, his mouth explored her body. Thorn kissed her all over as he fed his hunger. He sensed her body climb higher toward release, and he wanted to join her.

He pulled away from Ivy and slid off his pants, joining her again on the bed and pulling her into his arms. He brushed her long hair back from her face and kissed her forehead.

"This shall hurt, Ivy, but it will only hurt the first time. I would take the pain myself if I could, but I can't. I will be as gentle as I can. Do you trust me?" Marcus asked.

"Yes, Marcus. I trust you always."

Marcus reached down and stroked her again, sliding his finger inside her, in and out. As her passion built for him, she tightened around his finger. After he pulled his finger away, he gently slid himself inside her.

She stiffened in his arms at the intrusion. He realized he would hurt her, and it pained him, after he pushed past her resistance, he could show her unbelievable pleasure. The kind of pleasure that was one of a kind and could only be shared together.

He lowered his head and whispered, "Trust me, Ivy," as he kissed her deeply. She ran her fingers through his hair to pull his head down for his kiss. She deepened the kiss to distract herself from the pain.

As Ivy relaxed against him, Marcus slid all the way inside her, filling her completely. He closed his eyes and leaned his forehead against hers, calming himself to keep from taking her too fast. Marcus placed a gentle kiss on her lips as he began the sweet decent into pleasure.

He slid in and out of Ivy, moving his body slowly and gently with hers. He listened to her moan as he gazed into her eyes. When he saw her eyes fill with passion and heat, he moved faster. She watched him as she moved her body along with his and held onto his arms as the passion overtook them both. He didn't know where he began and she ended. They became one together, as they were always meant to be.

As Marcus gently made love to her, Ivy became whole. She had never experienced this connection with anybody but Marcus. Ivy moved her body with his, clinging to him as he made love to her. She felt the pressure build in her body and didn't know what was happening to herself, but she trusted Marcus to ease the ache that consumed her. Ivy pressed herself tighter to his body and clung to him, kissing his chest and moaning his name. She needed to release this pressure.

Marcus could feel Ivy tighten around him, her body strung tight. He quickened his pace, Ivy matching him thrust for thrust. Ivy screamed out his name as her body opened for him, and he let out a roar as he thrust into her, deeply filling her with his love. Their bodies floated back onto the bed in a sea of wonder.

As Marcus pulled out of her, he wrapped her in his arms, her head under his chin. She placed a soft kiss on his chest and whispered his name.

"Oh, Marcus," Ivy sighed as she drifted to sleep.

Marcus held her and listened to her soft snores as she slept against him. He tightened his arms around her and whispered, "I love you, Ivy." He placed a kiss on the top of her head.

He would let her sleep for now, but as soon as she woke, he would get his answers. They were running out of time. This was the last thing he should have done; he didn't have time for this. When he opened the door, he had every intention of getting to the bottom of all his questions. But as he saw her standing there naked, he changed his mind. Making love to her suddenly became his number one priority. He smiled as he thought to himself that he did not regret it one bit. He tightened his hold and waited for Ivy to wake up.

Chapter Eight

IVY SNUGGLED INTO THE warmth of Marcus's body as she awoke from a wonderful dream. She'd dreamed Marcus had made love to her. As she opened her eyes, she noticed she was lying naked in Marcus's arms. She raised her eyes and saw him watching her. She felt herself blush all over.

"It wasn't a dream?" Ivy asked.

Thorn laughed. "No it was most definitely not a dream." He hugged her as he lowered his head and gently kissed her on her lips.

"How are you, my darling?"

"I feel wonderful," Ivy replied as she stretched her body alongside his.

"Wonderful enough to answer a few questions?"

Ivy looked away and she shook her head no.

"Ivy, your time is up. I need the answers to my questions now. We won't be rising from this bed until you tell me what I need to know."

Ivy tried to pull herself out of Thorn's arms, but he only tightened his hold on her. He would not let her run from him anymore. Ivy felt trapped with nowhere to go. His hold was like iron bands wrapped around her. She could not sway him any longer, but she at least had to try.

"I need you to trust me, Ivy. You trusted me enough with your body, now trust me with your heart."

"I can't, Thorn. I won't ever allow you that trust again."

"I understand I hurt you in the past, but it was not our time then."

"And I suppose it is now?" Ivy asked.

"It is complicated, Ivy, but we will figure it out. I must know who abandoned you in the sea. I realize this involves Charles."

"Charles and I will figure it out. We don't need you."

"Oh, but you do, Ivy. You see, there is a ship following us, and if I am not mistaken, I think it is the ship you came from. We will cross paths with them any time now."

Ivy went pale at this bit of news. Thorn wouldn't give her over to them, but if she didn't tell him something, then he would let the ship catch them. It would be out of her control on what happened next. She had to stall as long as she could to protect Charles. He depended on her, wherever he was.

"Should I help you out with this and make it a little easier for you?"

"How would you accomplish that?"

"Let me see. This involves Charles and a smuggling ring in Margate. Am I correct?"

"How are you aware of this information?"

"Ivy, just because I haven't been back to Margate in the last seven years doesn't mean I am unaware of what happens there or with you," Thorn stated.

"Why would you care what was happening with me?"

Thorn shook his head. "You still don't understand, do you?"

"Understand what Thorn? I received your message loud and clear that day in your mother's garden. Even if I didn't, you were plain as day when you told me you didn't love me after I confessed my love for you."

"That was the hardest thing I ever did, Ivy, but it was in your best interests."

"It devastated me, Thorn. I was heartbroken for years. But those memories are in the past. I am over you. After I escape this mess with Charles, I will move on. I will find myself somebody who will love me, and I will marry him and start a family."

"It didn't seem like you were over me a couple of hours ago."

Ivy laughed. "Oh that. That wasn't love, Thorn. That was lust. Another thing I learned from you. I don't love you anymore."

If Ivy spoke the truth, those words would cut Thorn deep, but he knew Ivy lied to him again. He understood by the expression in her eyes. For now, he would let her keep her lies. He would break through her defenses later when she was safe. At this moment, he needed to get his answers and keep her safe.

Ivy waited for Thorn to argue with her. But he said nothing. She tried to hurt him like he'd hurt her, but she didn't get a reaction from him. She wanted him to suffer as she suffered all those years go. Maybe she could heal if he suffered as she did.

Thorn slid out of bed, pulled on his pants, and walked over to his desk. He slid the drawer open and pulled out a letter. Ivy recognized the crest on the back of the envelope. It was the Mallory seal. *Where did he get that from?* Ivy wondered.

Thorn slid the letter out of the envelope and read the letter aloud.

Dear Thorn,

The town of Margate needs your help. I can't say much in case this letter falls into the wrong hands, but it is regarding the matter we discussed when we saw each other last year—about some neighboring ports. The matter has moved itself to Margate, but on an escalated scale. The people of Margate are not safe. Also, I fear for Ivy's safety. She is curious of the ships' activities near the coves and my involvement with them. She wanders too close. I beg of you to please return and see to her safety. Captain Shears has taken an interest in her. You understand what dire consequences that will entail.

Your friend for life,

Charles Mallory

Thorn looked from the letter to notice that Ivy had turned pale. He wanted to comfort her and set her mind at ease, but time was not on their side anymore. He needed answers now before the other ship caught them, which would be any moment.

"When did you receive that letter?" Ivy whispered.

"Six months ago," Thorn answered.

"Where have you been? Why didn't you come to help sooner? We needed you, and you weren't even going to come home, were you?"

Ivy pelted him with question after question, and his guilt rose within him. She spoke the truth. He didn't want to return in the beginning. The truth was he didn't want to come anywhere near Margate or Ivy. He had his reasons for not returning to Margate. He was still angry at his father for keeping Ivy and him apart. But in the end, he couldn't allow Ivy to become involved with any kind of danger. The captain Charles spoke of was dangerous. Thorn needed to be honest with Ivy as much as he could. If he wanted to gain her trust and have her be honest with him, then he must repay her in kind.

"No, I didn't want to return to Margate. I thought Charles could control the situation. He had done it before," Marcus told Ivy.

"What do you mean before?"

"Charles is an Intelligence Officer for the Crown. He has been in this situation before and knows how to follow procedures. The only difference in this assignment was that he had a sister to keep his cover from. A sister, mind you, that is too curious for her own good. A sister who put her brother's cover and life in jeopardy with her curiosity."

"What was I supposed to do? There were times he came home dressed in rags and sporting shiners. When I questioned him, he told me to mind my business and that it was nothing to concern myself with."

"Then that is what you should have done. You should not have gone investigating on your own. Especially around the coves. You know how dangerous it is there. Is that where you were captured?"

Ivy didn't answer him. Thorn glared as she tightened her lips and crossed her arms across her chest.

"Answer me, Ivy. I need to know what happened. Time has run out for you."

Ivy shook her head in denial. She couldn't betray Charles. Thorn said Charles worked for the Crown, but how was Ivy supposed to believe him? None of this made any sense. Ivy walked back and forth across the cabin floor as she tried to understand this new information on her mind. If Charles worked for the Crown, then wouldn't he have been away all the time like Thorn was? Why did Charles have secret meetings with the awful sea captain? Ivy ran into the captain in town once, and he made her uncomfortable. Then there was the night they captured her. Ivy saw Charles giving the captain money at the local tavern. They were drinking and laughing together. Ivy confronted Charles outside the tavern, where he told her she witnessed nothing and ordered her home. The captain noticed them talking and thought he had been double-crossed, so he set his men on Charles, beating him. Ivy watched in horror and screamed at them to stop.

The captain only laughed as he grabbed her, threw her over his shoulder, and carried her to his horse. He climbed his horse while still holding Ivy and galloped away. Ivy saw the captain's men kick Charles in his side one last time before they jumped on their horses and followed.

Ivy didn't know how badly they'd hurt Charles, but he'd never got up to chase them. They kept her on the ship for two days before they set sail. During that entire time, Charles never attempted to rescue her. She overheard conversations about Charles while they kept her captive. Nobody had seen him. The captain had sent his men out to find him with orders to kill him for double-crossing them. They tried to get her to talk about her connection to him, where he might hide, and who he was. Ivy refused to talk to them. They withheld food from her and kept her tied in the captain's cabin. She shuddered as she thought about being stuck in his dirty, smelly cabin. The rats that ran across the floor, eating the scraps of food littered about. That wasn't even the worst of her ordeal. The captain himself was a force to be reckoned with. Just the thought of seeing him again made Ivy shake.

Chapter Nine

THORN SAW IVY SHAKE and grow paler as the minutes ticked by. He strode over to her and pulled her in his arms. He held her close, and her body relaxed into his. She released a huge sigh and rested her head against his chest.

"Talk to me, Ivy. Let me help you," Thorn pleaded with her.

"Oh, Thorn, it was horrible. They attacked Charles and kidnapped me. I don't even know if Charles is alive. I overhead them say they didn't know where he was. Don't let them take me again," Ivy begged Thorn as she looked at him and grabbed his arms. Her fingers clenched around his hard biceps.

"Start at the beginning," Thorn urged.

Ivy told Thorn how the ships came into Margate, sneaking into the coves late at night. It would only be one ship at first, every couple of months. Then more ships arrived sometimes on a weekly basis. The villagers gossiped about smuggling. During this time, Charles acted differently. He would come and leave at strange hours and was unaccounted for during many times of the day. Whenever Ivy questioned Charles, he told her he worked on something for their father. So, Ivy questioned their father, and he informed her it was nothing for a lady to be worried about and too busy herself with the house.

When Charles snuck out one evening, Ivy decided to follow him. He dressed himself as a dock worker. She followed him to the coves. Once he got there, he would row out to one of the ships. He carried a bag when he boarded the ship. He was only on the ship for an hour, and when he left, the crew loaded his small boat with a couple of crates. Ivy didn't know what was inside those crates. She followed Charles a half dozen more times, and the same scene played out before her. The last time she trailed Charles, he'd caught her spying on him. She had fallen asleep by the horses awaiting his return from the boat. He lingered on the ship longer than the usual hour. He was furious with her but didn't make a scene because he realized the captain's men shadowed him. Charles hid Ivy in the bushes as he got rid of the men. Then he took Ivy home.

When they reached Mallton Manor, he took Ivy into their father's study and locked her inside. He then went to wake their father and told him what had happened. Both men came into the study and demanded her silence on what she observed. They also informed her she would leave for London in the morning and that she had no choice. Ivy begged and pleaded with them, telling them she would not follow Charles anymore. Her father told her it didn't matter. They worried for her safety and she would be safer in London. It was time she settled. She was to find herself a groom this season. They would make arrangements with Katherine, Thorn's mother, in the morning. They directed her to her room for bed and to rise early in the morning to pack. The carriage would be waiting to take her to London.

Ivy continued to her bedroom, furious with them for controlling her life and for hiding what was happening around Margate. She heard the rumors and whispers. The villagers thought her family was involved in the treason. The worst part was, she believed it to be true. How was she to defend her family's honor if she wasn't certain if there were truth to the rumors?

Ivy arrived in London the next day, and Katherine met her. She confided in Katherine about her fears, but Katherine was evasive and tried to calm Ivy. Katherine distracted Ivy with shopping trips and invitations to balls. But it was at a ball that something intensified Ivy's doubts and fears. She was hot from the overcrowded ballroom, so she took a stroll along the balcony. She rested on a bench in the shadows and that was when she overheard a conversation about Charles and Margate. The gentlemen planned a terror plot with Charles at the center of it. Ivy needed to return to Charles and warn him. After the men left the balcony, Ivy snuck into the ballroom and located Katherine. She told her a lie of having a headache and begged to go home. When she arrived home, Ivy packed a small bag and left it hidden in the wardrobe. The next morning when Katherine came in her room to check on her, Ivy pleaded to stay home to rest. Katherine agreed and left for the morning. Ivy snuck away from the house with her bag and caught a hackney to the mail coach. She rode on the mail coach, headed to Margate.

After she reached Margate, she waited in the village for Charles to arrive. She watched him go into the tavern and waited for him to leave. When he did, she ran to him and told him of the terror plot against him. She was arguing with him when the captain and his men left the tavern. They noticed Charles holding her by the arms and got suspicious of him. He ordered his men to attack Charles. The captain grabbed Ivy and left for his boat. Ivy watched helplessly as they beat Charles. She cried for his mercy and tried to fight, but the captain was too strong.

She described how the captain had kept her captive in his cabin. How they questioned her over and over about her association with Charles.

They didn't believe her when she told them she knew nothing. She told Thorn about the cabin and the rats. Ivy described how they withheld food and water after a few days. They thought she would talk if they starved her. She told him how shocked she was when the captain knew her name and where she lived. How he recalled her life. He'd ordered his men to follow her when she was in the village because she'd caught his eye. Ivy informed Thorn about Tommy the cabin boy, how he brought her scraps of food. But during the whole ordeal, she never told them anything. She would never betray Charles.

"How did you get out to sea in the lifeboat?"

"I only remember bits and pieces."

She continued to tell Thorn the last thing she remembered was how the captain tried to touch her, but she fought him. Then the captain laughed and told her that in time she would beg for his touch. When he tried to kiss her, Ivy bit him. That enraged him, and he slapped her across the face, which sent her falling across the floor. She recalled hitting her head against the door. After that, her memory scattered into pieces. She woke once when a sailor lifted her and carried her across his shoulders like a sack of potatoes.

They threw her into the lifeboat, and the captain laughed about dropping the boat into the sea. She was a problem they didn't need to worry about anymore. Ivy cried out, but the thunder drumming through the clouds swallowed her cries. She looked and noticed Tommy shaking his head for her to be quiet. She heard the captain laugh as he slapped the cabin boy on the back and ordered him to take care of the ship's stowaway. The crew laughed at his jest. The cabin boy moved to the lifeboat and whispered to Ivy how sorry he was. He explained this was better for her, compared to what he had seen the captain do to pretty ladies before. He lowered the boat in the sea. Ivy recalled the lifeboat landing on top of the waves with a force that knocked her backward. She hit her head again, this time on the seat. The last thing she remembered was lying her head on the seat as rain pelted against her, then she slid her eyes closed.

"Then when I opened my eyes again, I saw you."

Thorn pulled Ivy back into his arms again, hugging her body close to his. His arms tightened around her harder. Ivy let out a groan, and Thorn relaxed his arms. He slid his hands to Ivy's face and cupped her cheeks, lowered his mouth, and devoured her lips. He kissed her with anger, then with relief, then with a softness that made Ivy cry. She could tell from his kiss the different emotions he experienced. Ivy returned his kiss, matching his emotions kiss by kiss. Thorn felt the tears as they slid along Ivy's cheeks, running past his fingers straight to his heart. He wiped the tears from her face and rested his forehead against hers.

"You are safe now. I won't let anything ever happen to you."

"But what about Charles? Do you think he's alive?"

"Yes, I believe Charles is alive. I think he's in hiding, and I know the place. We will find him, but first we must rid ourselves of this ship following us. They must have discovered that you are alive and want to finish the job they started."

"What is inside those crates? How is Charles involved with them?"

"They are guns for the French. They have organized families along the coast posing as refugees. When the time comes, those families who have sought help from the English will turn on us and bring the war to our shores. Margate was a perfect town for them to smuggle their goods into, with all the hidden coves. Charles said they found places to store their goods in our private caves. He stumbled across them by chance one day," Thorn explained.

"He went to the Home Office and informed them what was occurring in Margate and how he'd heard rumors from other neighboring ports of the same activity. Then the Crown wanted Charles to go undercover to discover their plot. They wanted him to pose as someone who worked for a prominent family in the area. A family whose ideas were sympathetic to the French and angry with the English government about their current laws. He was to become a trusted ally, learn where they distributed their supplies, and which families were involved in the plot. From what I gathered from my contacts in the Home Office, Charles had a list of the families involved and discovered where the storage facilities were for the weapons."

"I ruined it, didn't I?"

"Well, you didn't help matters."

"What about the terror plot I overheard at the ball?"

"There are aristocrats in England who want the attack to happen. They must have found out what Charles accomplished and made a plan to stop him."

"Why would any English man or lady want the war to happen on our shores?" Ivy asked.

"There are gentlemen of rank who are dissatisfied with Parliament. Also, many members of the ton are broke. They are being paid money to turn their backs on what is going on in their own villages. If these attacks happen, then they could get out of debt and move their own agendas in Parliament," Thorn explained.

"Why didn't you come back to Margate sooner, Thorn? Charles needed you, Margate needed you, and I needed you."

"I thought he could handle it and you. Obviously, I was mistaken."

Ivy pushed out of Thorn's arms.

"I don't need to be handled."

"Oh, that is where you are wrong, Ivy dear. But from now on, it will be my job, and I don't intend to fail at it."

"How is it your job, Thorn? I can handle myself."

"We will get married, Ivy. Once this ship lands in Margate and we find Charles. Charles and I will bring down this plot, then you and I will get married at Thornhill Manor."

"I'm not marrying you, so clear yourself of that idea this instant."

"You shall, darling. You see, you are ruined. Not only by sleeping with me, but by being kidnapped by a shady captain. Word would have spread all over London about the dire consequences you have gotten yourself into. Since, I have come to your rescue and will deliver you home safely, your family will feel indebted to me for your safety, and your father will insist we marry. And since I will inform him of my intentions and that you have refused, he will answer for you, and we shall be married."

"You have not asked," Ivy stated through clenched teeth.

Thorn smiled at Ivy, the smug smile saying he didn't have to ask.

Ivy stomped her feet over to the desk and sat in the chair. She refused to fight with him. If he couldn't ask her like a proper gentleman and confess his undying love for her, then she would not marry him. She would run away where he couldn't find her. Ivy would deal with that problem later.

Thorn watched Ivy pout in his chair. He kept smiling at her, laughing in the inside. He had her where he wanted her. She would be his for the rest of their lives. He understood she wants to be romanced, and he would in time. But now was not the time. There would be plenty of moments later, and romance her he would. She wouldn't know how to react when he attempted to impress and charm her. Now they needed to get out of their current predicament, return to Margate, and straighten out the mess Charles had gotten himself into. He didn't want to raise Ivy's hopes, but he thought had an idea where Charles was hiding. It was a private cave they'd discovered when they were boys. Ivy knew nothing about it. Of all the times she followed them, this was the one place she never found them. Thorn prayed that Charles was alive.

There was a knock on the door. Screams came from the upper deck.

"Captain, come quick, the ship following us has reached us. Their captain wishes to come aboard," Sammy yelled through the door.

Thorn flew open the door, grabbing Sammy by the collar. "I thought I told you to hide us?"

"We didn't have time for that Capt'n. Their ship sailed like it was being carried on a breeze toward us," Sammy explained.

"Is it who I think it is?" Thorn asked.

"Yeah, Captain, and he knows who you are."

Thorn pulled on the rest of his clothes and laced his boots. He then went to the wall and pulled his sword down and strapped it to his body. When he moved toward the door, he threw out instructions before he left.

"You stay here with her and guard her with your life, Sammy. Let nobody into this cabin except for me. No matter what she tries, you are not to let her out of this cabin," he ordered.

Thorn then turned to Ivy. "As for you, you stay put. If I am going to convince him we do not have you, and you are to stay out of the way. Do I make myself clear?"

Ivy sat in the chair and did not reply to him. She would not make him any promises. She needed answers about Charles, and this captain was the only one who could help her. Ivy realized nothing would happen to her with Thorn around. He would protect her. As soon as she could, she would make her way on deck.

"Promise me, Ivy. I don't have times for games."

Ivy refused to answer.

Thorn pulled Ivy from the chair and kissed her roughly. He wrapped her tightly into his arms and urged her lips apart with his tongue. His tongue stroked inside her mouth, dominating her senses. When he pulled away quickly, he tipped her face so her eyes to meet his.

"Stay," he commanded. He ran from the room and up to the deck.

Chapter Ten

THORN CLIMBED TO THE top deck to see another ship alongside his. The crew of both ships stood armed, ready to fight for their captains. As he stalked to the edge of the ship, his fingers tightened their hold on his sword, ready to draw battle at any moment. The other captain yelled for permission to board his ship. Thorn agreed for him to come aboard. He told his men to stand down but remain guarded.

Thorn watched as the Captain Shears ran across the plank between the two ships. For an older man, he still moved with ease. His age showed though from when Thorn first had the misfortune of meeting him. He battled him in war and wits many times over the last few years. But the captain's hard living took a toll on him. Thorn had seen for himself how he enjoyed his food and wine, and his belly showed proof too. Still, he moved with a swiftness that kept Thorn on guard.

Shears came aboard and walked over to Thorn, extending his hand in a gracious manner. Thorn stood in silence, not offering his hand in return. This would be no friendly meeting.

"Greetings, Captain Thornhill, what a surprise to see you in this area of open sea. This isn't your usual course to cruise upon." The captain laughed to himself.

"I am on my way home for a brief visit. Is that all right with you, Captain Shears?" Thorn asked.

"Of course. The sea is open to anybody who dares to travel upon it."

"Well, I dare."

"You are from the seaside village with the coves. What is the name of your charming town? It seems to have slipped my mind."

"Margate, as you are well aware," Thorn answered.

Captain Shears laughed, "Ah yes, a charming village full of charming maidens. One in particular caught my eye there recently."

Thorn tightened his hold on the sword. His fingers dug into the hilt, wanting to fight the captain. He knew Shears baited him about Ivy, but he wouldn't succumb to his taunts. If he would get anything out of this meeting, he needed to keep his temper under control. He let Shears continue to talk, with the knowledge he would slip on any clue for him to help save Charles. When he thought of all Ivy endured in his capture, he wanted to slice right through him.

"You might know her—long blonde hair, eyes the color of England's grass, a body to make a man want to love for hours on end."

"You are describing half the women of England, Shears," Thorn said through clenched teeth.

"Ah, but not one who also shares the name of your ship, Captain Thornhill. Are you on your way to visit her?"

"Where and whom I visit is no concern of yours. Would you like to tell me why you have been following me the past few days?"

"I seem to have lost some baggage during that fierce storm a week ago. Perhaps you saw it floating around and rescued it."

"What kind of baggage?" Thorn asked.

"The stowaway variety."

"How do you lose a stowaway, Shears?"

"Well in a fit of anger, I might have dropped it out to sea in a lifeboat. I thought it was dead but was informed it was very much alive after the storm. Well, I felt awful for leaving a stowaway in a horrible storm with no protection that I had to return to rescue it. But when we found the lifeboat, it was empty."

"Why trouble yourself for a stowaway?" Thorn asked.

"I think any man would trouble himself for this stowaway. Did you happen to come across any lifeboats on your way back home, Captain?" Shears asked.

"No, I can't say we have."

"Not that you would tell me if you had, but I thought I would at least try."

"What business are you doing in Margate? That's not your usual route," Thorn questioned.

"I have expanded my route to many ports along your English borders. My goods are in high demand," Shears bragged.

"You are to stay out of Margate and never return. I will not have your kind soiling the area."

"That is not for you to decide. It is not against the law to sell my wares."

"Yes, it is actually."

"But Captain, the good people of Margate and surrounding villages like my goods."

"Your goods are illegal, and I will put a stop to you."

The captain laughed. "Like how your good friend Mallory and his lovely sister, Lady Ivy, attempted to?"

"Do not speak her name."

"Ah, a beauty like no other. She was the one I described to you. The goddess with the long blonde hair you want to run your fingers through."

Thorn advanced on the captain and wrapped his hands around his throat. His fingers tightened around Shears's neck, cutting off his air. He watched as the captain's face turned red and felt his hands clawing at his to stop. Thorn's crew pulled him off Shears, not wanting to start a fight with Shears's crew.

Captain Shears grabbed his throat, rubbing the life back into it. As he struggled to get his breath back, he pulled out his sword and advanced on Thorn. Thorn saw him coming and pulled out his sword, clashing it against the captain's. They deflected each other's blows with accurate precision. They fought the length of the deck with the skill of warriors.

~~~~~~

Sammy shut the door and busied himself straightening the captain's room. His cheeks turned bright red, too embarrassed to look at Lady Ivy after he witnessed her and the captain's passionate exchange. What he didn't realize was that Ivy herself was just as embarrassed.

Ivy could not dwell on the uncomfortable moment. She needed to leave the cabin. She must get herself on deck to hear what Thorn discussed with Captain Shears. Ivy was also afraid for Thorn. She heard rumors of how Shears harmed innocent people, and she wanted to make sure Thorn was safe. Ivy couldn't allow anything to happen to him; she needed his help.

Ivy either needed to think of a plan to escape or to convince Sammy to release her. She was never one to use her charms to her advantage, but now was the time to put them to use. Over the years, she witnessed the way other girls persuaded anyone from a footman to a gentleman to do their bidding. It wasn't as if Ivy didn't know how, she just didn't like to deceive anyone. It wasn't the time to be polite, it was a time for desperate measures.

"Sammy, I have eaten nothing since breakfast. Can you bring me a snack while we wait for Thorn?" Ivy asked in a sweet, innocent voice.

"Ah, lass, you know I'm not supposed to leave you for anything. Wait for the capt'n to return."

"I will lock the door when you leave and only open it for you. Also, I wondered if you knew where my dress was. I would like to get dressed." Ivy continued to use her charms on Sammy and hoped he would bend to help her.

"Well, miss, the captain had to cut away the dress, being as how it was soaked to your skin." Sammy turned red.

Ivy ran out of ideas. She had to get on deck soon. Sammy followed orders too proficiently. Since he wouldn't leave the cabin, Ivy needed to distract him so she could sneak away. She wanted to learn of any news of Charles.

Ivy saw the tea set sitting on the table and decided she found a mess for Sammy to clean. She walked over to the table and swiped her arm out, knocking the tea set to the ground. It shattered into many pieces, scattering across the cabin floor. She gripped the edge of the table with her hands and closed her eyes.

"Oh my, I feel light-headed. I am so sorry for the clutter, Sammy," Ivy wept.

Sammy rushed over and steered her away from the broken glass, leading her to the bed.

"Now, now, it's all right. Only an accident." He patted her on the arm trying to comfort her. "You sit here and let old Sammy clean this mess. Are you okay, lass?"

"I am a little dizzy. I will be fine if I rest here." Ivy felt horrible for lying to Sammy. He was a gentle, sweet old man. She didn't wish to deceive him but knew no other way.

"Not surprised with what you have suffered."

Sammy walked over to the mess to clean the broken glass. Ivy slid off the bed and tip-toed to the door. She glanced over her shoulder to see if Sammy noticed that she'd moved from the bed. He was busy talking as he swept all the tiny pieces, not noticing her disappearance. Ivy slid the door open and escaped into the passageway. She ran to the stairs when she heard Sammy calling her name as he dashed after her. She continued up the stairs to the top deck and kept moving toward the shouts and the sound of swords clashing together. Ivy increased her pace as her heart pounded rapidly in fear for Thorn.

She ran right into the middle of the fight between Thorn and Captain Shears. She came to a halt as a sword slashed past her ear. Ivy froze in fear. Soon her body shook, but she couldn't move. Thorn acted quickly and pulled her behind him as he pointed the tip of his sword against Shears's heart.

Captain Shears laughed. "Ah, it seems you have found my lost piece of baggage after all."

Shears looked over Thorn's shoulder and leered at Ivy's state of undress. While Ivy ran on deck, Thorn's shirt rode up her legs, showing off a good portion of her thighs. When she glanced down her body, Ivy noticed she had not buttoned the shirt all the way. She yanked the shirt down and buttoned the shirt to her throat.

Thorn nodded his head at his men to take Shears. As his men disarmed Shears and pulled him away, Thorn turned around to check on Ivy. She shook from fear and from the sight of the man who captured her. He was furious with her for coming above but admired her courage. Thorn wrapped her in his arms to calm her.

He lowered his head to her ear and whispered, "I thought I told you to stay below in my cabin. Do you never listen?"

"I needed to come on deck to find out if Charles is alive."

"I told you I would handle it, Ivy."

"By killing him?" Ivy asked

"I wasn't killing him."

"Are we having a lovers' spat?" Shears shouted across the ship.

"I will get rid of him. I need you to keep quiet while I handle this."

"Shears, I will be kind today and let you live. Get off my ship and stay away from Margate," Thorn shouted.

"I have some unfinished business in Margate. When I have it cleared up, I will leave and not a moment before," he threatened.

As Shears left the ship, he looked over his shoulder at Ivy. He stared at her, then at the name written on the side of the ship and gave her an evil smile.

"Well from the looks of things you must really be his mistress of the sea," he laughed as he swung back to his ship.

"What did he mean by that, Thorn?" Ivy asked.

"Nothing. You need to return to the cabin before I have a different kind of mutiny on my ship. My crew haven't been near a port for a while, and you are a distraction they need not admire. Also, I don't want to kill any of my men for looking at you dressed as you are."

Ivy blushed as she grabbed the shirt and held it tighter to her body. She ran back to his cabin, just as quickly as she ran to the deck. When she rushed into the cabin, she found Thorn's coat lying across the trunk. She wrapped it around her body to shield it from everyone, including Thorn.

Chapter Eleven

THORN FOLLOWED IVY AT a much slower pace and ran into Sammy on his way to the cabin.

"I'm sorry, Captain. She tricked me. You know I'm a softie when it comes to tears."

"Don't let it happen again, Sammy. We will be in danger of Captain Shears and many others before we finish this assignment. We shall protect her, even from herself. Get on deck and sail us home to Margate as fast as you can."

"Aye, Captain. We should be able to guide her into port in a couple of days."

As Thorn strolled into the cabin, he noticed Ivy had wrapped his woolen coat around herself as a shield. Did she think it would stop him from touching her? She had a lot to learn about him before she would be his wife, but she had plenty of time to learn in the coming months. It would be a joy to teach her.

"Why did you let him go? Did you discover any news on Charles?" Ivy asked.

"I couldn't keep him. He would have given instructions to his men to attack us if he didn't return. I will not risk the lives of my men for him."

"What about Charles?"

"Charles is still alive."

"Where is he then?"

"I don't know, and neither does Shears. Since he did not boast of his kill, then Charles is alive and in hiding. That is why he returned to the boat to retrieve you, to use you as leverage."

"Leverage for what?"

"To draw out Charles and kill him. And after he finished with Charles, he would have had his way with you and then killed you too. He would leave no witnesses to his destruction. You were to remain in this cabin and not to be seen."

"I had to find out about Charles."

"All you did was give Captain Shears your whereabouts. Now he will follow us and try to find an opportunity to capture you again. The next time I order you to stay put, you will follow my directions."

"You do not own me, Marcus Thornhill. I will go wherever I please."

"When we return, you will become my wife, and I will own you. Then you will go nowhere without my permission."

"I will not marry you."

"Oh, you will, Ivy darling, and there will be no stopping it."

"That is what you think," Ivy said.

She continued to fight him on the subject of marriage. She needed a keeper considering all the dangerous situations she kept putting herself in. When she ran into the middle of the sword fight, his heart dropped to the bottom of his stomach. His sword barely missed slicing through her. Not to mention, when he found her on that lifeboat, he felt like his entire world had ended until he saw her shallow breathing and realized she was still alive. He spent too many years fighting this attraction. Ivy would be his for eternity and now was the moment to convince her she was his.

Thorn walked to Ivy and peeled his coat away from her soft skin. He slid it off her shoulders to pool around their feet. Then he started to unbutton his shirt. But Ivy would have no part of it.

"What do you think you are doing?" Ivy swatted his hands.

"I think you know, my dear. If not, let me show you," Thorn replied as he ran his tongue across Ivy's lips, slipping inside to kiss her deeply.

Ivy tried to close her lips to resist, but her emotions could not fight him. She moaned softly as she parted her lips to allow his tongue to slide inside. When his tongue swept inside her mouth to stroke against her tongue, Ivy gripped his arms and clung to him. Her legs buckled before Thorn lifted her into his arms, carried her to the desk, and placed her among his papers. He continued kissing her as his fingers worked to finish unbuttoning his shirt.

He pulled away from their kiss as he peeled the shirt from her body. While he slid the shirt away, he gazed upon her. Thorn ran his fingers over her shoulders, along her arms, and back up again. Then he glided them across her collarbone and slipped them lower to her breasts. He brushed his thumbs gently across her nipples and watched as they tightened into firm buds from his touch. His hands palmed her breasts as his fingers stroked her nipples. He heard Ivy moan and glanced upward from her body into her eyes. Thorn noticed them turning to a darker green with desire.

"You are so beautiful, Ivy. I could stare at you like this for hours."

Ivy blushed unable to speak. Marcus's hands did things to her body that heated her, as if she could melt into a puddle on his desk. She didn't understand what to do. She only knew she wanted Marcus to continue to touch her and never stop.

"Oh, Marcus," Ivy moaned.

Marcus leaned in and took a nipple into his mouth, softly sucking it between his lips. His tongue swirled around the nipple until it hardened tighter against his lips. Ivy ran her fingers through his hair and pulled his head closer to her breasts. He placed soft kisses across to the other nipple, softly kissing it, and then licked around the nipple before he sucked it deeper into his mouth. Ivy arched her back into his mouth and pressed his face closer to her chest. As he made love to her breasts, he slid his hand lower across her belly, then to her heated core. He could feel the heat coming off her in waves.

He slid his hands between her thighs to open them wider as he slid his body in between them. His fingers traced a path along her thighs as he moved to the center of her heat. His fingers barely touched her skin as they glided up and down her thighs. He continued this teasing game, touching her heat then back to her thighs. He built her need so she would come undone for him.

When she bucked against his fingers, he realized she was losing control. He slid his finger deep inside her, her wetness soaked it. He sucked on her nipples harder as his finger moved inside her faster. Thorn felt the pressure tighten inside her when she pulsed around his finger. When her nails dug into the muscles of his arms, he realized Ivy was almost ready to explode. He pulled his finger out of her and moved his mouth to her lips for a soul-searching kiss.

He wrapped his hands into her hair and gathered her closer to deepen the kiss. Ivy pressed her body into Marcus's. She needed his touch, his kiss. She needed him to help ease her ache. She wanted so much more from him. Ivy desired to be one with him again.

"Please, Marcus, I need you."

"I know Ivy. I need you just as much. But I wish to fulfill a dream I have imagined ever since I saw you sitting at my desk in nothing but my shirt."

He lay Ivy back on his desk, spread out for his delight. Thorn spread her legs open wide and lowered his head down to her heat. Ivy gasped his name as she tried to pull away. But he held her thighs apart as he softly stroked his tongue over her wetness. He pressed his mouth against her center, brushing his tongue back and forth as he tasted her sweetness.

His kiss mortified Ivy. It wasn't proper. But her senses became electrified at the first stroke of his tongue. It felt like heaven. His tongue stroked her at the center of her core and made her feel things she never experienced before. As her body pressed into his mouth, Ivy reached below and feathered her fingers through Marcus's hair. Marcus lifted her legs to his shoulders as he continued to make love to her with his mouth.

Marcus sensed the exact moment Ivy enjoyed the pleasure of his tongue. Her body pressed into his mouth, and her center became wetter. His tongue stroked her core faster and faster, and then he slid his fingers inside her deeply. Her pressure climbed higher as his fingers stroked in a rhythm with his tongue. Marcus slid his mouth over her clit and softly sucked as the pressure built. He felt Ivy ready to fly over the edge, so he sucked harder, his tongue licking between his sucks. Ivy bucked against his mouth as he sent her over the edge. His mouth kissed her wetness one last time as he slid up her body.

As he kissed her on her lips, he pulled out his hardness and slid inside her. Ivy's eyes opened, and she gasped as he filled her completely. Marcus moved in long, slow strokes and watched the desire in Ivy's eyes as he moved inside her. She wrapped her legs around his hips as he slid as deep inside her as he could go. Then he paused and rotated his hips in a circle against her core as she tightened around him. Ivy gripped his shoulders as she pressed her body against him. When her nipples brushed against his chest, he growled her name and quickened the pace.

Ivy needed him so much. She kissed his neck, shoulders, and chest as Marcus moved inside her at a slow, intense pace. She wanted more, she needed more. Ivy pressed herself tighter against his body. Her hands moved all over him, wanting to touch him everywhere. She wanted to drive Marcus as crazy as he made love to her. When she touched and kissed him, she heard him growl, and he stroked inside her faster. She moved her body with Marcus's and squeezed her hold on him. Her ache intensified again, and she needed to find release. Her fingers dug into his back, and she moaned his name as the pressure grew to new heights, seeking its release.

"Marcus," Ivy moaned.

"Ivy," Marcus roared as he joined Ivy in her release, his seed entering her body in completion.

Ivy sagged against him, her arms wrapped around his neck as she placed soft kisses against him. He gathered her closer into his embrace.

"I will never finish my work at this desk ever again," Marcus teased, tipping Ivy's face to his for a kiss.

He kissed her softly as he carried her to his bed. He slid on the mattress and held her in his lap. Marcus tugged the covers over them as he settled against the pillows.

"It serves you right for taking advantage of me like that."

"I wasn't taking advantage I was trying to persuade you, my darling."

"Either way, the answer is still no."

"I think your final answer will be yes, but I see I still have more work to change your mind."

"Marcus …"

"I don't want to argue now, Ivy. I only want to hold you."

Ivy didn't wish to argue either. She lay her head against his chest and kissed him from time to time as her fingers traced over the scars on his body. She didn't want to ask how he received them because it would show how much she cared. But she worried how he had gotten them. Was his life ever in immediate danger? How did he escape? Ivy wondered many questions about the last seven years of his life. Since she would not ask him about his scars, she caressed them and hoped it would pacify her curiosity.

When Ivy traced his wounds, he wanted to share with her about the battles he fought that scarred his body. But he understood she wasn't ready to hear of the danger he had been in, and he wasn't ready to tell her. There was more danger to come, and he didn't wish to frighten her. When she kissed his scars, he became hard again and was amazed at the emotions she entranced within him. They finished making love, and he was already ready to love her again. Ivy drifted to sleep as she placed soft kisses across his body. He pulled her in closer and wrapped her tighter within the blanket.

He would never get enough of her. His love for her grew stronger and stronger. He now understood why his father wanted him to leave her alone all those years ago. She had been too young to deal with their emotions, and in some ways she still was. He realized it was part of the reason she refused to marry him. He must take their union slower. Thorn needed to get himself under control.

He owed his father an apology when he returned to Thornhill Manor. His father only tried to protect them. Ivy was too young to deal with Marcus away at war. She needed to experience her youth and all it entailed. She deserved a chance at the London season, with the balls, picnics, and outings. She didn't need to be closed off from life, to sit at home, worrying if he would return to her alive or not.

He knew his father thought of Ivy like a daughter, as did his mother. His mother was the one who sponsored Ivy during her seasons in London. It was through his mother he learned how Ivy blossomed into womanhood and how sought after she was. He heard about her gentlemen suitors, her dances at balls, and her carriage rides in the park. Whenever he read a letter from his mother, he had to control his jealousy. He should have been the one to dance with Ivy, to ride in a carriage with her, to charm her with flowers.

When he received the last letter from his mother, he knew it was time to come home to Ivy. He had avoided her for far too long. His mother told him of a gentleman who wooed Ivy and how close Ivy had grown to her suitor. She feared Ivy would marry this other gentleman, and he agreed. His mother urged him to return home and to make Ivy his wife. So, he swallowed his pride with the intention to make amends to Ivy, hoping she would become his bride. Who knew these circumstances would fall into his lap? He would woo her after the vows. The main concern was for her safety, and the only way to achieve that was to make her his bride as soon as possible.

Chapter Twelve

IVY AWOKE SLOWLY TO FIND she was alone in bed. She looked around the cabin. Marcus wasn't there. She rolled over to her side and ran her hand over the pillow where Marcus had lain. Her hand dipped where the indention of his head rested. She pulled the pillow to her body and hugged it tightly.

"Oh, Marcus, where do we go from here?" Ivy whispered to herself.

As Ivy lay in his bed, she wondered how this would turn out. She realized she would have to marry him. It wasn't as if she didn't want to; it was not how she pictured their wedding in her mind. She dreamed over the years that when Marcus returned home from the war, he would confess his undying love to her. Then he would court her, charm her, and marry her for the entire ton to witness. Ivy knew they gossiped about her waiting for him. They said when he came back, he wouldn't want her because she was too young and naïve for him. Marcus would want a mature, sophisticated woman, not a mere girl. But Ivy never gave up hope he would return to her.

But she never imagined in all her dreams the incredible passion they would share. She never dreamed the touch of his hands on her would make her desire him to such amazing heights. When he kissed her, all she thought about was him and the feelings he ignited within her. As she lay there with images of his touch and kisses, it made Ivy wish Marcus was still beside her.

She wanted to show him what his touch did to her, but most of all, she wanted to drive Marcus to the same level of desire that consumed her.

Ivy decided she would marry him, but she would not make it easy. Nor would she sit at home and wait for him. She would help him locate her brother. Then after they found Charles, she would persuade him to love her. Deep down, he must love her. Their passion couldn't be so strong without love, could it?

Ivy missed him. Not from their lost years, but from his absence now. She wanted to be in his presence. She wanted him to hold her and tell her everything would sort itself out. She decided to go look for him. They had wasted enough time, and she didn't want to waste another moment.

She threw back the covers and climbed out of bed. As she moved to the wash basin, her body felt tender. She realized their lovemaking made her use parts of her body she'd never used before. Ivy slid her hand along her body where she ached and smiled to herself. It was well worth it. Ivy glanced at the desk, and her body blushed as she remembered their lovemaking. The way Marcus loved her was so delicious. She realized she wanted to learn more, and Marcus could show and teach her. So, Ivy hurried to get dressed.

Ivy sponged her body clean and went to Marcus's trunk for a clean shirt. As she dug through the trunk, her hand brushed across a book. Ivy pulled it out and realized it was a book of poems she lost around the time Marcus left. She opened the first page and saw her name written across the page as she always did with her books. When Ivy flipped through the book, she noticed the pages she turned down at the corners of her favorite poems. The pages were worn and had been handled many times. Marcus must have read the book a lot. She came to the back cover of the book, where a red rose rested against a handwritten poem. The poem was written in Marcus's handwriting inside the back cover.

Ivy My Love

Your love is like a vine

Forever clinging to my heart.

It tangles in between my jagged thorns.

I try to break apart

To free myself from your love,

But you have grown so heavy in my thoughts.

I will let you go for now

For you need to grow wild and free,

But I will return to you with my love,

And our love will cling forever between the ivy and the thorns.

A tear slid along Ivy's face, followed by more. She wiped them away with her fingertips. The poem was beautiful. He had loved her all those years ago. Why did he deny his love to her after their kiss? Why didn't he tell her? Ivy glided her fingers across the words on the page, touching the power of them to her soul. She wanted to ask Marcus about the poem but realized she couldn't. She didn't want him to think she'd looked through his belongings. She slid the book back where she found it. When the time was appropriate, they would discuss the poem. For now, she was content with the knowledge of Marcus's love for her.

Ivy found a blue shirt and slid it over her body. She dug through the trunk and located a cravat to use for a belt. Ivy wrapped herself in a blanket, left the cabin, and wandered the ship until she found Marcus laughing with Sammy on the quarterdeck. Ivy paused to watch him; he seemed much younger and carefree when he laughed. He always could make everybody around him enjoy themselves in his company. If he didn't charm the ladies of the ton, he was a man's man to the gentlemen. He could make the shyest debutante a beautiful bloom after one dance. A drink or a game of cards would win over any gentleman. How Ivy envied his ability to fit in any situation, even commanding a ship.

Marcus glanced across the deck and noticed Ivy watching him. He continued laughing at Sammy's joke but did not take his eyes off her. He saw her the moment she walked on deck. Marcus sensed her near him and waited for her to join them. But when she didn't, he needed to look. He couldn't seem to get enough of her. She looked charming as she stood there wrapped in a blanket. He only hoped she wore something underneath it.

When his eyes met hers, Ivy smiled shyly at him. He smiled back at her and nodded his head for her to come over to them. She slowly walked to join him. He slid his arms around her and brought her close to his body.

Sammy knew he lost the captain's attention when he noticed that Thorn wasn't even looking at him, but over at Lady Ivy. When the lass joined them on the quarterdeck, he realized he was no longer wanted. He shook his head and wandered away. He was happy for him. The captain had been alone for a long time and sometimes wore a lost stare. Over the years, he never sought the company of tavern whores or any lady. Now Sammy understood why.

They stayed wrapped in each other's embrace for a long time. Neither one of them spoke for fear of ruining the moment. Marcus kissed her on the forehead and turned her in his arms as he leaned against the railing. He snugged the blanket tighter around her as he brought her back into his body.

He leaned to whisper in her ear, "Look at the stars, Ivy."

Ivy titled her head to gaze at the star-filled night. There wasn't a cloud in sight to block the glazing starlight. The sky was a midnight blue filled with millions of stars twinkling down on them. They appeared to wink at her. Ivy lay her head against Marcus's chest as she watched the stars with him, feeling a sense of contentment before the next storm. They stayed locked in their embrace for an endless moment of time. She didn't want to ruin this moment but wished to understand.

"Marcus?"

"Did you know every chance I got I would gaze at these stars and imagine you? I wondered where you were and what you were doing. Also, I wished upon them to be with you."

Ivy turned in his arms and gazed into his eyes, the color of the night sky.

"Why?" Ivy asked.

"You still don't get it, do you? I realize I have confused you over the last few years and the last few days, but my feelings for you have never changed, except to grow stronger."

"What are those feelings Marcus?" Ivy didn't want to raise her hopes, but she started to realize that she didn't imagine those feelings of belonging to each other.

Marcus reached to slide Ivy's hair behind her ears. His fingers traced them and then slid to hold her cheeks in his hands. He leaned over and softly brushed his lips across hers. His kiss was as soft as the gentle breeze that blew around them. He parted her lips with his tongue and kissed her deeply. His kiss was full of his love for her. He drew away from her lips and looked deep into her eyes.

"I love you, my sweet Ivy," Marcus whispered.

A tear slid along Ivy's cheek, and Marcus brushed it away with his finger. He watched the emotions play across her face. When her eyes softened with her love for him, he knew she forgave him for his past lies. One day he would explain why and hoped she would understand, but for now he waited to hear her speak the same words to him.

Ivy had waited to hear these words for years. She sensed his love in his kisses and touch. She heard the love in his voice when he spoke those sweet words to her. It was all she ever wanted to hear. It didn't matter why anymore. The only thing that mattered was that he loved her. She smiled at him and brushed his hair back as she ran her fingers through the ends of his hair.

"I love you, Marcus," Ivy whispered in return.

Marcus grasped her to his chest and bent his head to kiss her deeply, in a kiss Ivy felt to her toes. She wrapped her arms around his neck and held on as she kissed him with all the love she held for him. She took over the kiss and slid her tongue between his lips into his mouth. As she traced her tongue across his teeth, she explored his mouth, tasting him. Ivy relished in her sense of security of acquiring his love and she kissed him with her soul. When she opened her mouth to his, she kissed him all the kisses she missed giving him over the years.

Ivy's passion astounded Marcus. She kissed him with so much pent-up emotion that he let her show him her love by these kisses. He could taste her love for him with every stroke of her tongue against his. He could sense her need for him. Thorn would always regret denying her the love they could have shared all these years. But until the day he died, he would redeem his love to her every day.

Ivy drew away from the kiss and brushed her lips across his. She opened her eyes and stared into his stormy blue eyes, which spoke of his need and love for her. She smiled as she ran her fingers back and forth across the whiskers on his face. Ivy enjoyed the roughness of his face on her fingers and body.

Marcus removed her hand from his face, wrapped them between his fingers, and brought them to his mouth for a kiss.

"I need to shave."

"No, you are perfect," Ivy whispered.

She suddenly felt shy and didn't understand how to act. She had known Marcus all her life, but they had never confessed their love to each other before. Ivy was afraid to ruin the moment, for fear he would take his love away. She never wanted to lose it again. Ivy knew she was silly. He took her virginity and had made love to her twice now. But she still felt shy. She reached with her other hand to slide her hair behind her ears.

Marcus laughed softly at Ivy's shyness. Any other man wouldn't waste a minute on her innocence. They would want a lady who understood the score. He had acted that way before, but he didn't want a sophisticated lady of the ton. He wanted his sweet maiden whose innocence rained down upon his soul and washed away all the evil. Marcus wanted to enjoy her sweet nature for the rest of his life.

Marcus also realized from the kiss they shared there was a temptress underneath all her sweetness. He would enjoy exploring her desires and teaching her the passion they would share. Marcus understood Ivy could be stubborn when she wanted to be. But he knew the tricks to break through her stubbornness. She might resist at first, but she would never deny them their love or passion for each other.

He still needed to take it slow with her, as her emotions were still vulnerable. They still had much to accomplish as they searched for Charles and put Shears out of permanent commission. With all the commotion, they needed to get married. Not only because they loved each other, but because she needed his protection. Ivy was a target now more than ever. Shears had a powerful benefactor in England who paved his way in vengeance. He thought Charles was onto whoever it was. He must keep Ivy safe, and marriage was the only answer.

Not only was there the threat of Shears, but Ivy's reputation would be ruined in the ton after her ordeal reached the gossipers. They would shun her from every drawing room to ballroom. She needed his name for her protection too. He was a marquess and next in line to a dukedom. With his name, no one would dare to slam a door in her face; they would bow at her feet for her kindness. None of them would ever deserve it because his Ivy was a better soul than all of them combined.

"Do you want to help me steer her?" Thorn asked Ivy as he slid her along his body and let her toes touch the deck again.

"Her?" Ivy asked.

"Yes, her," Thorn chuckled.

"Should I be jealous?"

Thorn kept smiling. "No, not at all."

"Does she have a name?"

"*My Hedera.*"

"What does that mean? Is it Latin?"

"Yes, it's Latin. I'm impressed you know."

"Who do you think helped Charles study? He was horrible at languages. Father would get so angry with him."

"I never knew; he always seemed to pass his exams."

"Well, of course. I'm an excellent tutor." Ivy smirked.

"Shall we see if you are an excellent student too?" Thorn distracted Ivy from the name on his boat. He wasn't ready for her to learn its meaning. It was another discussion they would share when it was time.

For some reason, Thorn did not want her to understand the meaning of his boat. She wondered why? As soon as she returned home, she would locate Charles's old Latin school books and search for the definition of Hedera. Ivy decided to drop her curiosity for now and discover the underlying cause of it later. Everything was too fresh to delve into with new dilemmas.

Thorn guided Ivy to the ship's wheel. He placed her hands on the wheel and covered them with his own. Thorn huddled his body close against Ivy's backside, his hardness pressing into her back.

He leaned and whispered into her ear, "Do you feel her power underneath your hands? Do you feel how she guides you to your destiny but still needs you to control her path?"

Ivy leaned into Thorn and lay her head against his shoulder. She listened to his voice murmur in her ear as he described the ship. Her body became liquid as his voice soothed her soul. She closed her eyes as she wondered if he spoke about the ship or herself. Was that how he felt about them? Ivy became drowsy as he ran his fingers up and down her arms and clasped his fingers between hers on the ship's wheel. His voice lulled her to sleep as his gentle voice echoed his love for his ship on the open sea.

As Ivy drifted to sleep, Thorn smiled and admired her with her head lain against his shoulder and her lips slightly parted. Even though she had fallen asleep, her hands still clasped tightly between his on the ship's wheel. He wanted to wake her with a kiss and make love to her on his deck, but knew they had no privacy. He lifted her in his arms, placed a kiss on her forehead, and carried her to his cabin. She needed her sleep, for the future would be demanding.

Chapter Thirteen

A FEW DAYS LATER IVY was having tea and eating more of the delicious pastries the cook had prepared for her when Marcus entered the cabin. He sauntered over to Ivy and placed a kiss on the top of her head.

"Did you sleep well, my dear?" Marcus asked.

"Yes, Marcus. Do you want some of these?"

Marcus smiled at her fondly. "No, you may eat them all."

Ivy smiled at Marcus as she bit into the last pastry and licked the icing from her fingers. As innocent as the action was to Ivy, it made Marcus silently groan with desire. She held no clue how it affected him, and he didn't have the time to show her. They were to arrive into port in an hour, and their families would wait for them to get off the ship. He sent Jake ahead to make arrangements. He also needed to maneuver Ivy off the ship without any unwanted attention. The last thing he needed was to get caught with his pants down around his ankles.

As Ivy smiled at Thorn, she noticed he'd changed out of his captain's gear and into the attire of an aristocrat. He wore tan trousers tucked into black Hessians. His hair was groomed back and tied with a dark blue ribbon that matched his waistcoat. His cravat was neatly wrapped around his throat. While he was handsome, Ivy preferred him as a sailor. This Thorn was too serious and did not return her smile.

"Ivy, we will sail into Margate within the next hour. I have made arrangements for my carriage to meet us at the dock. I do not know if our families will greet us, but I expect Mother will be too excited to wait. A letter has been sent to your father to inform him I have you safely on board. My man has brought back clothes for you to dress in. I will leave you to your privacy to change."

Ivy listened to Marcus talk, unsure of his sudden change of behavior. He became serious after he first greeted her good morning. She didn't know who to react, afraid he'd changed his mind from a few nights before. Perhaps he felt forced to give her his name. She didn't want him this way.

"Everything will be all right, Ivy. I will explain the situation to our families." Marcus misunderstood her silence as a change of mind.

Ivy, unsure where Marcus's mind was, nodded her head.

He gazed at her for a few moments as he drank in her loveliness and wished he held the answers for her. He realized this would be their last moment alone together until they wed. Why did she stay silent? Did she regret their confessions of love? Marcus's mind went crazy at her silence and knew there was only one action he wanted to take.

He went to her and pulled her from the chair into his arms. He tilted her head and kissed her hungrily. His mouth devoured her lips with his love. His tongue stroked the fires against hers and their passion came alive as she kissed him back as hungrily. She gripped his arms and moaned into his mouth as he drank the love from her lips. As quickly as he pulled her to him, he released her and turned to walk out the door as Ivy clutched the desk for support. Her knees wobbled.

Ivy brought her fingers to her bruised lips and touched where his lips left their mark. She didn't understand what to think of his visit. She was more confused than ever. She jumped when a knock sounded on the door.

"Lady Ivy, may I come inside, lass?" she heard Sammy shout from the other side of the door.

Ivy walked to the door on unsteady legs and opened the cabin to Sammy. She held on tightly to the panel as he came in with a dress thrown over his arm and a small bag.

"These are for you, miss."

"Thank you, Sammy, you can lay them on the bed."

"The captain wanted me to tell you we will dock in half an hour and for you to be dressed."

"You can tell the captain I will be ready soon."

"He also said you are not to come on deck until he returns for you. He worries for your safety."

"I will await him here. Thank you, Sammy, for the care you have given me. Please, thank Anton for the wonderful food too," Ivy said.

Sammy turned a bright red at her praise and bowed to her.

"It has been our pleasure, my lady." With a wink, he walked out of the cabin.

Ivy sighed as she drifted to the bed and held the day dress Sammy laid on the bed for her. Katherine sent one of her dresses for Ivy to wear. It was a beautiful blue day dress with white lace around the end of the sleeves. She also sent a pelisse to wear over it. Inside the bag, Ivy found a white chemise, silk stockings, and a pair of heels. Ivy's hand brushed across a bottle at the bottom of the bag and pulled it out. She smiled when she saw that Katherine sent Ivy's favorite perfume. Ivy opened the bottle and breathed in the beautiful scent of roses. It smelled heavenly, and Ivy relaxed. She dabbed the scent on her wrist and behind her ears.

Ivy slid off Thorn's shirt, letting it drift to the floor. She dressed in the clothes Sammy brought her. It felt so wonderful to get dressed. She bent over to gather Thorn's shirt and brought it to her nose to breathe in his scent. Ivy knew as much as she was glad to wear dresses, she would miss wearing his shirt and feeling a part of him against her body. She laid the shirt across his trunk and walked over to the desk with her shoes and stockings. As she slid the stockings along her legs, she experienced the cool touch of the silk stroking her thighs. It was the same sensation as Thorn's hands when he caressed her as he made love to her. She sat down to place her feet in the borrowed shoes. Ivy rose to shake out her skirts when Thorn walked into the cabin. She stood still as she waited for him to speak.

Thorn stood inside the doorway and admired Ivy in the blue dress he asked his mother to send for her. She looked as lovely as she did when she stood in the garden all those years ago. He realized he confused her earlier with his strange mood. He'd received bad news from Jake when he had returned from his errand of gathering the clothes. Charles was still missing, and he didn't know how to inform Ivy. Also, his father sent a missive that described the men who watched Ivy's home. He must get Ivy off the boat without being seen, and she could not return home. She would have to stay at Thornhill Manor until they wed. He also needed to keep her there so she didn't escape to find Charles on her own. He counted on his mother to keep Ivy busy with wedding plans and the betrothal ball.

"I will miss seeing you in my shirt."

Ivy blushed as she looked down and picked at the lace on her dress. "I will miss wearing it."

"Will you?" Thorn asked.

"Yes."

Well then, I must make sure it is all you wear after we exchange our vows. However, I like it better when you wear nothing at all."

Thorn laughed as Ivy continued to blush.

"I will never grow tired of your blushes, my dear, especially since I discovered you blush all over."

"Thorn, you are such a naughty tease," Ivy flirted back.

"You have seen nothing yet, but you will once we are married."

"Do you still want to marry me?" Ivy asked quietly as she bent her head, afraid to hear his answer.

Thorn walked to Ivy and tilted her head so her eyes could meet his. He wanted her to see the answer in his eyes as well as hear it from his lips.

"Yes, Ivy, I still want to marry you. I love you with all my heart. I understand this is not how you dreamed of my proposal. It is not how I wished to ask you either. I wanted to court you, to shower you with gifts, to take you for rides in the park, and to dance every waltz with you at a ball."

Ivy could see the love in Marcus's eyes as he told her he loved her. She felt more secure with his answer than she had this morning.

"I love you too, Marcus. But you never asked me."

Marcus laughed as he gathered Ivy in his arms and swung her around in circles. Ivy clutched onto his shoulders and laughed with him.

"So, I never asked, did I, minx? Well, I will just have to remedy that, won't I?"

He sat Ivy in his chair. Thorn knelt on the floor by her knees, reached for her hand, and brought it to place across his heart.

"My sweet Ivy, will you do me the greatest honor and become by bride? I promise to love and cherish you forever,"

"I will Marcus, and I promise to love and cherish you forever too."

Marcus pulled Ivy from the chair and hugged her to him.

"You have made me the happiest man on earth," Marcus told her as he leaned over to kiss her sweetly on the lips, sealing his promise to her.

He held her in his arms and sat on the chair with her, tucking her close to his body. He rested silently with her for a time as he stroked her hair along her back. They sat content and understood this would be the last time someone would allow them to be alone together. He needed to tell her about Charles.

"Ivy I am sorry to have to tell you that Charles is still missing. I have word from your father he has not seen Charles since the night you disappeared."

Ivy turned in Thorn's lap with tears in her eyes.

"Where could he be, Marcus? Do you think he is dead?"

"I don't know, honey. They have not found his body, so that is a promising sign. If they killed him, they would have displayed him like a trophy. I will search for him as soon as I have you secured at Thornhill Manor."

"But I want to see my father, and won't people gossip if I reside with you before we are wed?"

"You will see your father. The rest of the people can hang; I won't be able to look for Charles if you are not safe at Thornhill. Everybody knows how close you are to my mother, and they will be told you are planning the betrothal ball and our wedding."

"I want to help you look for Charles," Ivy told Thorn.

"No. I will not risk your life to more danger. You will not fight or disobey me on this. I cannot have you coming to any harm. I will not lose you after I have made you mine."

Ivy remained silent. She didn't like Thorn's directions on what she could or could not do. If this would be how their marriage worked, she would not speak those vows to him no matter how much she loved him.

Thorn took her silence as an act of defiance. This wasn't proceeding the way he planned. He had to convince her of the danger she was in and how he only wanted to protect her.

"Please, Ivy. Promise me you will stay at Thornhill and help Mother. You are in extreme danger of Shears and whoever works for him. Only Charles has knowledge of all the players involved. I need to search for him and stop the terror that holds England in her grip. I don't want to lose you."

Thorn kissed Ivy on the lips slowly, softly nipping at her lips with his. His tongue traced her lips, pulling her bottom lips in between his and sucking gently. Ivy opened her mouth to allow his tongue to glide against hers. Ivy was defenseless when he kissed her, and she would promise him anything if he continued his persuasion.

"Promise me, Ivy," Thorn whispered between kisses. His tongue swept in her mouth stroking in long slow strokes, a dance across her tongue. Ivy moaned and pulled his head closer, her tongue mimicking his. Thorn dragged his tongue back out, holding his mouth inches from her mouth as he teased her.

"Promise me, Ivy," Thorn whispered again as his tongue licked out across her lips, pulling back again.

Ivy moaned, wanting his mouth to devour her, needing his mouth to devour her. She hungered for him. She tried to pull his head down for more, but Thorn resisted.

"I promise, Thorn," Ivy groaned as Marcus swept her in a soul-searching kiss; teasing, tantalizing her senses with his kiss. His mouth consumed hers, drawing out her passion to join his in a sensual dance.

He gathered her closer to him and swung her around so that she straddled his lap. Her heat teased his hardness as he pressed against her core. His kiss became more desperate as she pressed down at the same time. He needed her heat wrapped around him. He slid his hands underneath her dress and stroked them along her thighs. His finger slid inside to sink into her wetness. He almost embarrassed himself at that sensation. Marcus realized he didn't have time to make love to her, but he needed her now more than he needed to breathe. He continued to stroke her heat, making her climb in need for him.

Ivy needed Marcus so badly but didn't know how to tell him. She did not want him thinking her some wanton hussy who always craved for him to make love to her. She moaned into his kiss as her body moved against his fingers with a mind of its own. Marcus's hardness pressed into her thighs as she pressed down on this finger. She knew he wanted her. Ivy's body tightened for release, and she moved faster against his hand.

Marcus could feel Ivy near release, and his own body needed to join hers. He pulled his hand and mouth away from her body and slid her further up his chest. His lips licked at the outline of her tight nipples through her dress and sucked them. As he savored her nipples, he unbuttoned the front of his trousers and pulled out his hardened cock. He needed to slow down. He wanted to take her fast and hard but understood it would be too much for her to handle. Ivy clutched at his head to press him into her breasts.

Marcus pulled away, and watched Ivy as he slid her down his body and entered her in a smooth quick thrust. He desired to watch her reaction as he slid into her wetness and to see her eyes darken green with a passion she never craved before. Her gaze did not disappoint him as her eyes widened with astonishment as he slid to the hilt of her heat. Marcus watched her eyes darken more as he circled his hips grinding into her slowly. He held onto her hips as he pressed upward.

Ivy tilted her head back in ecstasy as Marcus pushed inside her. She moaned as her breasts pressed forward. She didn't realize it was possible to make love this way. It felt so magnificent, and her body craved more. Ivy gazed at Marcus and saw the dark heat in his eyes—and the encouragement. She slowly rocked back and forth and heard Marcus groan louder. She took it as a sign she pleased him and decided to try more. Ivy slid her body up a little and slowly slid back down. His hardness slid in and out of her as she did this. Marcus's hands tightened at her waist. Ivy began a slow rhythm of this movement and felt every inch of him deep inside her heat. She wanted more though, she needed more, and she craved more. She increased the rhythm as she moved faster and came down harder.

This drove Marcus beyond madness with desire. He slid her dress and chemise off her shoulders and down her arms and bared her breasts to his added enjoyment. He palmed them in his hands, twisting her nipples as he bent his head. Marcus slid them into his mouth and sucked down on them as he tasted the tightness in his mouth. He needed more. He needed to take control from her but realized he couldn't. He must show her she held control in this relationship too. When he moved along with her rhythm, he let her control the pace as she pleasured him.

Her body tightened around him as her wetness gripped his hardness, pulsing around it. He knew she was close to losing control in his arms. He was ready to catch her when she did and join her in their release.

Ivy felt like she would unravel in his arms. She was on the edge; she slid down, feeling him deep inside her. Her hips moved around in a slow dance, rocking slowly back and forth as her core tightened like never before. Marcus sucked harder on her nipple, and she cried out as she exploded around him. Her body rocked against his as he pressed up harder inside her when he exploded. Ivy collapsed in his arms as she kissed him with little kisses along his chin.

Marcus gathered Ivy in closer to him. His soft touch as he caressed her gave her a sense of security. He let her take control of their lovemaking this time. She now understood why. He wanted to show her she would never have to lose her control. Sometimes she needed to let him be the one to have the control as he let her have it. She looked at him as she kissed him. He was still deep inside her.

"I promise, Marcus."

Marcus closed his eyes and kissed her gently on the forehead in relief.

"You are beyond beautiful, Ivy."

Ivy blushed at his compliment as she sensed the beauty of their love.

Marcus lifted her and sat her back in his chair. He walked to the washstand and cleaned himself. He wetted a towel and knelt in front of Ivy to slide the washcloth between her thighs as he washed her. Ivy hands shook as she straightened her dress over her shoulders. He stood and pulled her from the chair.

"Are you ready to go, my love?"

Ivy nodded her head, even though her legs were still unsteady from their lovemaking. She was nervous to see their families. She didn't want to shame her father or his parents with her behavior. Also, she hoped they wouldn't discover about how Marcus and she made love on his ship. She didn't want to be a disappointment those she loved.

Marcus wrapped his fingers through hers as he sensed her nervousness. He needed to reassure her that nobody would know of their lovemaking. Their secret would stay between them.

"Nobody will know Ivy; our lovemaking is only for our knowledge. Everyone will think we are getting married because I've realized I can't live without you. Now grace your face with your beautiful smile so we can reunite with our family."

Ivy smiled her shy, sweet smile that Marcus had fallen in love with all those years ago, laying her arm across his as he walked her out of his cabin. As they made their way to deck, he nodded to Sammy to put their plan of action into play. His crew moved around them to block Ivy from any prying eyes as they made their way off the ship and into his carriage. He wanted nobody to witness Ivy as she left his ship. Thorn did not want to subject her to any rumors or for their enemies to see her. He told her he would protect her at all costs, and he would not break his promise.

Chapter Fourteen

WHEN IVY STEPPED INTO Thorn's carriage, she saw her father and
Katherine waiting for them. She broke into tears as she went into her
father's arms.

"I am so sorry to have worried you, Papa," Ivy cried.

"It is all right, my child. All that matters is that you are safe now,"
her father comforted Ivy.

She cried into his jacket as he wrapped her in his comforting arms
and patted her back. She didn't think she would ever see him again after
Shears kidnapped her. When her tears ended, he reached inside his jacket
and pulled out a handkerchief she'd embroidered for him, with an M for
Mallory. He wiped away her tears like he did when she was little and would
get hurt from following the boys around in their mischief as she tried to
keep up with them. She clutched at his hand, not wanting to let go as he
eased her head to his shoulder. She sat there, secure in her father's love as
the carriage started for Thornhill.

Thorn stared as Ivy drifted to sleep in her father's arms. Her body
was exhausted from her ordeal and from his selfishness. He pushed her too
far with their lovemaking these past few days when she should have
recovered from her illness. In the weeks to come, he would keep his distance
from her in order for her to make a full recovery before their wedding. His

search for Charles and plans to stop a treasonous plot about to invade the shores of England would take most of his time.

Thorn would leave Ivy in the care of his mother. He could not keep his hands to himself when he was near her, and that was something he must do, especially if they stayed at Thornhill together before their wedding. His parents would not approve of anything more than him acting as a gentleman to Ivy, and she deserved no less from him. He continued to watch Ivy sleep and wished she was in his arms instead. As much as he desired her, he only wanted to comfort her now.

Katherine reached to lay her hand over Marcus's hand and squeezed his fingers. She saw the love her son held for the gentle, sweet girl across from them. For as long as she remembered, she thought of Ivy as her daughter and knew she would be one day. Marcus hadn't told them of his plans for Ivy, but Katherine assumed a wedding would soon be in the works. She realized Marcus loved Ivy all these years and that he'd stayed away for what he thought would be a sacrifice to Ivy. But Katherine also knew Ivy loved Marcus as deeply as he did her. She observed the girl with sadness in her eyes through the years as she missed him. Now the sadness would leave, and Katherine could watch their love bloom as she had seen when she witnessed their first kiss all those years ago.

Marcus looked at his mother's hand on his as she comforted him. She knew of his love for Ivy all these years, even though she never spoke of it. But he could hear it in her letters she sent him as she told him of the gentlemen who courted Ivy. Who Ivy danced with at the balls and who brought her flowers when they came for afternoon tea. He understood her intentions were not to make him jealous but to force him to confront his feelings. She wanted him to come home and act on them. He ignored the letters and told himself it was for the best, even though it really wasn't. He turned to his side and wrapped his mother in a hug.

"Welcome home, son."

"It is good to be home, Mother."

He continued to watch Ivy slumber as they journeyed to Thornhill. Nobody spoke of what needed to be said as they thought of the young girl who rested. Each one of them was deep in their own thoughts, all concerned about her.

But they were not the only ones who regarded the young lady. The tall, distinguished gentleman was leaned against the tavern as Thorn maneuvered Ivy into his carriage. He held admiration for Thornhill on the discretion of Ivy's identity as they left his ship. Anyone who walked or rode by wouldn't have seen a single thing out of the ordinary; but he waited for her. He felt relief at her safety and that no harm had come to her. When he heard of her abduction from the sea captain, he was furious. She was never to be harmed. Her life was at stake, and she was a threat to his operation. He would do everything in his power to keep her out of harm's way, but it appeared he would have help in that matter. But he couldn't recognize if it was help or competition.

The mysterious stranger strolled to his carriage and ordered his driver on a swift departure before they were seen. He wanted nobody to spot him in the area until he made his initial appearance. Now that he satisfied his curiosity with regard to the girl, he plotted his next plan of action to keep her safe.

Chapter Fifteen

WHEN THEY ARRIVED AT Thornhill Manor, Ivy still slept in her father's arms. Thorn stepped from the carriage, reached back inside, and swept Ivy into his arms to carry her inside. Ivy's father was about to protest when he felt the gentle pressure of Katherine's hand on his arm and the shake of her head to stay quiet. George Mallory sighed and released his hold on Ivy. Thorn nodded his head at George and gathered Ivy closer. Ivy snuggled into his arms but did not wake. George stepped from the carriage and helped Katherine to the ground. Katherine bustled past George and Thorn and ordered directions to the staff as they entered the manor.

"I have put her in the Rose Room, Thorn," Katherine directed Thorn where to go.

Thorn climbed the stairs to the bedroom wing of the house. Katherine followed at a discreet distance. They needed to follow the correct protocol now so no rumors would spread about Ivy. As much as Thorn wanted to be alone with Ivy, Katherine would not allow it until they wed. Katherine followed Thorn into the bedroom, watched as he lay Ivy on the bed, and pulled the quilt over her as he gently tucked her into bed. Katherine looked out the window and gave Thorn a moment alone with Ivy.

Thorn understood why his mother must stay in the room with him, and he thanked her for whatever privacy she allowed him. He sat on the edge of the bed, brushed the hair from Ivy's forehead, and leaned over to kiss her. His lips brushed her lips softly, lingering but for a moment. He watched Ivy's eyelids flutter open. When he saw her slight confusion, he reached for her hand. He noticed her about to speak when he squeezed her hand as he lifted his finger to her lips. Thorn nodded over at Katherine for Ivy to understand. He opened her hand and pressed a kiss to her palm. His lips lingered before he closed her palm to bring to his heart and then to hers and hoped she understood the meaning. He realized she did when she smiled sweetly at him and her hand closed tighter around the kiss.

Katherine turned to witness the exchange of love between her son and Ivy. She hated to end this, but Thorn had been in Ivy's bedroom long enough. It was time for him to leave before the staff started to talk. They needed to quell the rumors that floated around about Ivy, not create new ones.

"Thorn, your father and George are waiting for you in your father's study. I will take care of Ivy, dear."

Thorn nodded his head, walked over to his mother, and wrapped her in his arms.

"Thank you, Mother, for everything you have done." Thorn turned and walked from the bedroom.

Ivy watched as Thorn exited the room. She wished she could call out for him to stay with her but knew she couldn't. So much would happen, and she wanted his comfort through it all. She already noticed the distance he put between them. Ivy opened her hand after she squeezed it tightly and stared at it like she could actually see the kiss Marcus left. She raised her palm and pressed it to her heart to feel the power of the kiss to her soul.

Ivy raised her eyes to see Katherine watching her; she lowered her hand and swept it under the quilt. Katherine walked over to Ivy, sat next to her, pulled her into her arms, and softly stroked her hair. Ivy relaxed in her arms as she felt the love of a mother Katherine always gave her. They didn't talk, and Katherine continued to comfort Ivy, waiting for Ivy to confide in her like she always did. But Ivy became sleepy at the gentleness of Katherine's touch and drifted back to sleep. She wanted to tell Katherine what happened but was overwhelmed with emotion and she didn't know where to begin. She closed her eyes and sighed.

Katherine lay her back against the pillows and smiled at her sleeping form. She understood Ivy must have been through quite an ordeal. Katherine drew the quilt back over Ivy and she went to rest in the chair near the bed. She would watch over her like the daughter she could never have and protect her with her heart and soul. She would wait for Ivy to awake, ready to listen and offer her the comfort she needed.

Thorn strode to his father's study. The last moment he spent with his father was in the study. It would also concern the same subject they argued over all those years ago. Ivy. He now understood what his father tried to tell him. It didn't make it any easier, but he was no longer angry with him.

His father had thought Ivy was too young for him. He wanted Thorn to wait a few years when he was more settled with his life before he persuaded Ivy to marry him. His father stated Thorn still had a few wild oats to sow, and it wasn't fair to put Ivy in the middle. She was too young, sweet, and innocent for the wild life Thorn lived at the time. He knew both of his parents considered Ivy the daughter they never had.

Also, his father did not want his deep friendship with Ivy's father ruined because of a brief infatuation Thorn held for Ivy. He argued with his father what he felt for Ivy was real and not an infatuation. But his father witnessed how Thorn was with women and would not let him anywhere near Ivy to even hurt her. He argued Ivy deserved to enjoy the London season, to be courted by many men and to have her own choice.

Everybody realized how Ivy cared for Thorn. She had worn her heart on her sleeve, but she was too young to truly understand her emotions. It wasn't fair for Thorn to build upon those feelings and then leave her. Because, leave her he would in the end. He already made his commitment to his country by leaving to fight in the war that tore his country apart. He wanted Ivy to wait for him, even though he knew it wasn't fair for him to do so. Thorn searched for her in the garden because he was angry with his father from their fight. He needed her gentleness to soothe his soul before he left. After the kiss they shared, it only made him want more. But it was also the kiss that made him realize his father was correct. It was his anger toward his father that made him hurt Ivy like he did when he rejected her love.

He knew when he walked into his father's study he would see the same disappointment in his eyes. However, now he was his own man and could make decisions for Ivy and himself. He paused outside the door to draw a deep breath, laying his head against the heavy oak panel.

It was hard to leave Ivy like he did and not tell her how he felt. He wanted to reassure of his love but didn't want his mother to overhear what he wished to say. Before he could whisper words of his love, he remembered the promise he made to himself in the carriage about allowing her time to heal. Time she should have had on his ship, but time he didn't give her. He would let Katherine see to her comfort while he tried to find Charles and end the treason that invaded their shores. Thorn shoved open the door to the study and strolled in to confront Ivy's father and his.

His father stood near the fireplace with a glass in his hand and talked to George Mallory, who sat in a nearby armchair. Both men stopped talking when he walked into the room and watched him approach. His father reached behind him and lifted another glass off the fireplace mantle and handed it to him.

"You look like you could use one of these, son," Hamilton Thornhill noted.

Thorn reached for the glass and drank the fiery whiskey in one shot. He moved to the liquor cabinet, poured himself another and carried it over before he sank in the chair opposite of George. He nursed this drink a little slower as he waited for the questions to start.

"Thank you, Father, I guess I did."

"How is Ivy?" George asked Thorn.

"She is resting. Mother is staying with her. She will take good care of her."

"What happened to my girl, and how did you get involved? She is ruined from the rumors spreading among the ton."

"Those rumors are false, and Ivy is not ruined, nor will she ever be. We will marry and that is final."

"Explain yourself, Thorn," Hamilton said.

"I have asked Ivy to marry me, and she has consented."

"You have yet to ask my permission. You are not what Ivy needs. She needs somebody who will be home with her and make a family. Not somebody who faces danger on a ship at any opportunity he gets."

"I am what Ivy needs and what she wants. We love each other. I am resigning my commission after this last assignment. I will always be there for Ivy for the rest of our lives. Anyway, it is too late to ask for your permission. What's done is done and there is no time to delay."

"What do you mean it is too late?" George and Hamilton asked at the same time.

"I mean she is mine, and I have made her so." Thorn smiled secretly to himself as he remembered how he made her his.

George came out of his seat, red in the face, and advanced toward Thorn. He reached and grabbed Thorn's cravat to drag him toward him.

"Are you saying what I think you are saying? Did you ruin my precious daughter?" George asked Thorn angrily.

Thorn did not answer George. He would not tarnish Ivy's reputation. He did not see it as ruination. He saw it as a precious gift of their love for each other. Also, George deserved to be angry with Thorn. Ivy deserved better. The man must have been worried sick over Ivy, and he still worried over Charles. Only one of his children had been brought home to him.

"George, let him go. This will not solve anything. You know more than anybody else those two would marry eventually. It appears the time has finally come. Was it done the proper way? No. But Ivy will get the wedding she deserves. Hell, old man, we have been planning this since the day she was born," Hamilton said as he pulled George off Thorn.

Thorn rose, walked to the windows, and loosened his cravat. He stared outside as he thought of the right words to say to George to ease his mind. After he ran his fingers through his hair, he rubbed the back of his neck. He turned and walked over to George.

"George, I love Ivy with all my heart, and I promise to make every day of her life happier than the day before. Will you please give us your permission to marry?" Thorn extended his hand for George to shake.

"Yes, and if you don't hold on to your promise, I will make your life miserable in any way I can." George shook Thorn's hand.

Thorn nodded his head at George. Hamilton joined them to shake hands and offered congratulations.

"What a homecoming this is turning out to be. It is good to have you home. You have been away too long." Hamilton hugged Thorn.

"It is good to be home, Father."

"Well now that we have the business finished about finally making Ivy my daughter, let's get to the rest of this nasty business. What do you know about Charles's disappearance?"

Thorn sat again and explained to them on what Ivy told him about her disappearance and the last time she saw Charles alive. They discussed how Charles had yet to be seen and how they hadn't yet discovered a body. Thorn informed them about the run-in with Captain Shears and his threats toward Ivy. He gave directions on how he wanted Ivy under guard and that she was never to be alone. They all agreed her stay at Thornhill Manor was the best thing for her. Thorn outlined the places he thought Charles might hide, and at first light tomorrow he would set out to find him. They discussed the treason plot and the steps the Crown was taking to bring it to a halt. Thorn discovered more on how Margate became a central location because of its ports.

"What is the Crown doing to stop this from happening now that Charles is missing?" Thorn asked.

"As soon as we knew you were in port, I sent a message to the other agent involved in this. He'll be here in a couple of days. When he arrives, we will put together a plan to bring down Shears and the other traitors involved in this conspiracy," Hamilton explained.

"Who is this other agent? Can we trust him?" Thorn inquired.

"We don't know who he is, but Charles trusted him with his life. We sent word to the War Office to have him located and sent here immediately. He is the only other one who knows where the shipments are being held and the names of the families involved," George explained.

"Well, until he shows, I will try to locate Charles. Did you bring his papers with you, George? I will read through them to see if I can discover any clues."

"No, I didn't think about his notes. I was too concerned over Ivy to think about anything else. I will fetch them now and return for dinner. On my return, I will have Charles's papers, some clothes for Ivy, and her maid."

"Sounds like a good plan, gentleman. Shall we enjoy a good cigar before you leave? We need to celebrate, and you can discuss your plans for after the wedding, Thorn." Hamilton stood and walked over to his desk for his cigars.

Chapter Sixteen

WHEN IVY AWOKE AGAIN, her room was dark with shadows. The sun had set as the moon and stars shone in through her open window. Ivy sat in bed and looked around the familiar room. This was her favorite room at Thornhill Manor. They called it the Rose Room because it looked over Katherine's rose garden. During the summer you could smell the fresh roses from below. Ivy inhaled in the fresh fragrance and relaxed for the first time in days. This room, this house, always calmed her, and she felt safe here. She relaxed against the pillows and noticed Katherine sitting in the chair next to her bed. Katherine smiled at her.

"This has always been your favorite room, hasn't it?" Katherine asked Ivy.

"Yes, I've always loved this room."

Katherine rose from the chair and rested next to Ivy on the bed. She reached for Ivy's hand and gave it a gentle squeeze. She brushed the hair away from Ivy's face.

"How are you feeling, dear? You have been through such an ordeal."

Ivy, overcome with emotion from the last few days and the gentleness of Katherine's touch, started to cry. Too choked to speak, she laid her head on Katherine's shoulder and continued to cry. Katherine pulled her in close and as Ivy succumbed to her emotions. Katherine understood only a few of the details Ivy endured and realized she needed time to heal. She held her until Ivy calmed down. When Ivy drew away, she wiped her face with her hands. Katherine held out her handkerchief for Ivy to dry her eyes.

"Start at the beginning, my dear, and take your time," Katherine said, soothing Ivy.

"I am confused where to begin and where to end. So much has happened. So much is going to happen. I'm frightened but happy at the same time. Is that even possible?" Ivy asked.

"Yes, especially after what you have been through."

"Before I even begin, I want to tell you how sorry I am when I deceived you in London. I was desperate to reach Charles, and I should never have run away like I did. I never meant to worry you."

"Ivy, I forgive you. I am glad Thorn found you safe and could bring you home."

Ivy blushed when Katherine mentioned Thorn's name. It brought back the memories they shared on his ship. How was she to tell Katherine everything when most of her time on Thorn's ship was private? She knew Katherine would guess from the way Ivy blushed.

Ivy told Katherine of the conversation she'd overheard at the ball. She described how she made it back to Margate and the fight she'd with Charles that led to her kidnapping. Ivy told Katherine the horrors of her captivity on Captain Shears's ship. Then she mentioned the young boy, Tommy, who helped save her life.

"I don't know what the fates had in store for me, but they guided Thorn to find me. If it wasn't for him, I would have died, abandoned at sea. He even nursed me back to health on his ship."

"He was at the right place at the right time."

"Katherine, did you know?"

"Know what, dear?"

"That he loved me all these years."

Katherine nodded her head. "I thought he might."

"Why did you never say anything?"

"He never confided in me. But I always wrote to him on how you were. He fought his feelings toward you, but I wouldn't let him win."

"He asked me to marry him and professed his love."

"And what did you say?"

Ivy smiled shyly. "I told him yes, and that I loved him too."

Katherine let out a delightful laugh and pulled Ivy in for a hug.

"Well, finally. You will be my daughter at last. I didn't think my son would ever get around to asking you."

Ivy laughed along with Katherine. Her heart filled with joy as she shared her thoughts with Katherine. She was the mother she never had.

"I promise I will take good care of him, Katherine. I will make him happy."

"Oh, Ivy dear, don't you understand? You've always made him happy. I recognize how much you love him, and I take great comfort from that. Now, don't you think we can stop this Katherine business so you can start calling me Mother?"

"Yes, Mother."

"We have a lot of plans to make, my dear. We have a betrothal ball and a wedding to organize. How exciting this will be."

"We have to find Charles first. I cannot get married without knowing where he is."

"Of course, my dear. We will leave the search to the men, and we shall occupy ourselves with our plans. You leave everything to Thorn. He will locate Charles and settle this unrest."

Ivy stayed quiet and let Katherine discuss the plans for the ball and wedding. She would not stay out of the men's way on the search for Charles. She had knowledge of some of Charles's hiding places, just as Thorn did. To sit around and not help made her feel helpless. She could ride over their lands and look for Charles. If she didn't leave the estate grounds, then she wouldn't be in any danger of Captain Shears and his men. Thorn couldn't get mad if she took daily rides. Then she would feel like she was helping.

"Well, since we are on the subject of weddings, I should explain what happens on your wedding night. It can be a very beautiful union."

Katherine noticed the blush spread across Ivy's cheeks. When Ivy wouldn't look her in the eye, Katherine realized her son already gave Ivy her wedding night. She shouldn't be surprised. He'd wanted Ivy for years. Still, he should have waited, especially with how the poor girl suffered. She shook her head at her son's impatience.

"Well I guess from your blush, this talk is a little too late," Katherine observed. "I hope he was gentle with you, Ivy."

Ivy, too embarrassed to discuss Thorn's lovemaking, nodded her head in the affirmative.

"Well, since there is no more to say, I shall leave you to freshen for dinner. I will send Mabel in to help you change. Your father brought her over with your clothes. He would like to speak with you before dinner. I will see you downstairs, my dear."

Her father knocked on the door, and Ivy called for him to enter. He made his way over to the chair Katherine had occupied. He sat on the edge and drew her into his arms.

"You scared twenty years off my life Ivy, my girl," he gently scolded her.

Ivy returned her father's hug as tears leaked from her eyes.

"I am sorry for scaring you. I imagined none of this happening. Please, forgive me for everything."

"There is nothing to forgive, my daughter. All that matters is that you are home."

"Thorn will find Charles for us."

"I know he will. Thorn is the gentleman you want for a husband, isn't he? Do not think you are forced to marry him if you do not want to."

"It is my dream to marry him, Father. I love Marcus. I always have, you know that."

"I've only wished so much more for you."

"We love each other and want to build a life together, like the one you and Mother shared."

"Your mother would be happy for you. Katherine and she was planning this wedding while you were still in the cradle." George laughed.

"She will smile down from heaven when we say I do."

"Yes, I think she will, my dear. I miss her every day, but I always had you and your brother to help me through it. When I thought I lost you both it nearly destroyed me. I am grateful Thorn found you. But he found you only to take you away."

"Oh, Father, we will always be near. Plus, we will give you plenty of grandchildren to spoil."

"Well, I guess I can give you to him for those rewards in life you promise me."

"I love you, Father."

"I love you, my girl. Give me another promise to stay out of danger from here on out; my heart cannot take it."

Ivy laughed. "I promise."

George kissed Ivy on the cheek. "I will see you at dinner, honey."

After her father left, Mabel bustled in the room and talked a mile a minute. Ivy could not get in a word edgewise. She told her how everybody worried about her and searched for her everywhere. Mabel filled her in with all the latest gossip, especially the rumors surrounding Ivy's disappearance. Mabel helped her bathe and then dressed her for dinner. Ivy listened as she got ready. She didn't tell Mabel anything. She would not contribute to her own gossip. Mabel was sweet but also too friendly and liked to talk to anybody who listened.

When Mabel left, Ivy stood at the window overlooking the roses. She looked and saw the statue where Thorn kissed her all those years ago. She closed her eyes as she remembered his kiss from then to the kiss this morning. When she opened her eyes, she noticed Thorn leaned against the statue as he looked into her bedroom. She smiled at him, and he blew her a kiss. Ivy reached out her hand, grabbed the kiss and placed it over her heart. She blew him back a kiss, and he did the same as he laid his hand over his heart. Ivy realized then that all would be well.

She walked downstairs. Since it was only the family for dinner, they waited for her in the drawing room. Ivy's father talked to Thorn's father near the fireplace while Katherine and Thorn sat on the couch. They were all deep in conversation, and it appeared as if Katherine gave Thorn a lecture. Thorn glanced at Ivy as she walked into the room, smirked at her, and rolled his eyes at what his mother said. Ivy brought her hand to her mouth and giggled at the gesture. When Katherine realized Thorn wasn't listening to her anymore, she swatted at his hand, nodding toward Ivy. Thorn rose from the couch, walked over to Ivy, and escorted her into the room.

"Well, there is our lovely bride-to-be," Hamilton welcomed Ivy into the room.

He walked over to her and planted a kiss on her cheek.

"This moment deserves a toast." Hamilton nodded his head at the butler to pour everybody a glass of champagne.

After everybody held a glass, Hamilton raised his. "This has been a long time coming. We can't even describe how excited we are this is finally happening. Congratulations, Ivy and Thorn. Katherine and I welcome you into our family. Daughter."

"And I welcome you into our family, Thorn," George added.

"Ivy and I thank you for all your warm wishes." Thorn clinked his glass into Ivy's and placed a brief kiss across her lips.

Their parents cheered, and everybody sipped from their glasses. The butler announced dinner, and they went into the dining room to eat. As they ate dinner, they discussed when the upcoming wedding would take place. They agreed on the date, and the minister would read the banns on Sunday. Thorn's parents would hold the ball in one month's time, with the wedding the following weekend. They discussed they would act as normal as possible. It was not to be known Charles was missing or that any of them held knowledge of the treason. All their lives would be in danger if word leaked. They would portray to the masses that Ivy and Thorn were two eager, young people in a hurry to start their lives together.

Chapter Seventeen

WHEN IVY CAME DOWNSTAIRS the next morning, the breakfast room was empty except for Katherine. They said their good mornings and Ivy went to the buffet to choose her breakfast. The footman followed Ivy to the table to set her plate down and help her into her seat.

"That will be all, Thomas," Katherine said.

"Would you like some tea, dear?" Katherine asked Ivy.

"Yes, please."

Katherine poured Ivy her tea as Ivy ate. Katherine continued sorting her mail and regarded Ivy out of the corner of her eye. She understood this time to be overwhelming for the young girl, and she would need patience with her.

Ivy finished her breakfast and held the cup of tea between her hands as she savored the warmth from the cup. She wondered where Thorn was. She'd hoped to find him here and spend a few moments with him. If he had been here, she wanted to convince him to allow her to help in the search for Charles. She knew he would tell her no, but she hoped to persuade him otherwise. She didn't want to sit around and not help them.

"Has Thorn had breakfast yet?" Ivy asked Katherine.

Katherine glanced from her correspondence and smiled at Ivy.

"Yes, dear. The gentlemen woke hours ago. They have already set a plan of action for their search for Charles. Thorn took Pirate for some exercise and to search in some of their old hiding places. He should return for dinner."

"I wished to join him in the search."

"I think that is why he left so early, my dear. He knew you would ask, and he realized he could not refuse you. It is best if you stay close to Thornhill, Ivy. Your life is in danger."

"I understand, but I feel so helpless. It is my fault that Charles is missing."

Katherine came around the table and sat in the chair next to Ivy. She reached for Ivy's hands.

"It is not your fault, dear. Do not blame yourself. Our men will find Charles and end this madness. The best recovery for you is to stay put. That way Thorn doesn't have to worry about you while he is searching."

Ivy nodded her head as she agreed to stay put, at least until she was out of danger. As soon as it calmed down, she would find a way to help save Charles and the town of Margate.

"We have much to do today. We must put our heads together to plan your ball and wedding. Thorn is eager to make you his bride. I have sent my maid to London to bring Madame Levine to the estate to make your ball and bridal gown. We will leave the search to the boys and begin to make our plans."

That was how it continued for the next two weeks. Thorn and his men would search for Charles. Their fathers would talk to the local townsfolk and those from the neighboring towns to find out any information on future attacks. Katherine and Ivy planned the ball and wedding. The other agent still had not shown. They feared Shears discovered his identity and had done away with him. Only Charles knew the other agent's true identity.

Ivy didn't see much of Thorn, only in passing. He left before she awoke and rarely returned home until after Ivy retired to bed. Ivy still recovered from her sea ordeal and tried to wait for him. Usually, too exhausted, she would fall asleep before he arrived home. Twice, she snuck into his room and curled in his favorite chair before the fire to wait for him. However, the next morning she would find herself tucked into her own bed. She missed him, but most of all she missed being held in his arms. If Ivy didn't know any better, she would think Thorn was deliberately trying to avoid her.

When they saw each other, Thorn kept it formal and made sure a chaperone was in their presence. Ivy missed the passionate sea captain who'd swept her off her feet and into his bed. She missed him. She missed his kisses and his touch. He made her feel this unstoppable desire from him, and then he stopped his attention. Did he have second thoughts about a marriage to her? Did he feel trapped?

Ivy was angry at herself and him for making her insecure about their relationship. For years, she promised herself she would not give him her love again. Then all it took was her lost at sea and having Thorn find her. He broke down all her defenses on his ship, and she gave him all her love. She thought she held his love in return. But ever since they had returned to Thornhill Manor, he drifted away and confused her. It was hard to get excited with Katherine's plans when she wasn't sure if Thorn loved her. She wanted time alone with him to reassure herself. She only wanted to be held in his arms again and feel the touch of his lips against hers.

Ivy was in the garden cutting roses for the front hall when she heard the footsteps behind her. She rose slowly with a smile, hoping it was Thorn sneaking away to spend a few stolen moments with her. She smoothed the front of her green day dress as she turned. Her smile fell when she realized it wasn't Thorn.

"Well, that wasn't the greeting I was hoping for, lovely lady," the tall, dark gentlemen said as he strolled closer to her.

"I'm sorry, sir. I was expecting someone else."

"So, sorry to disappoint you, my lady." The gentleman bowed as he reached her.

Ivy laughed and shook her head at his silliness. Zane was just the friend she needed to see. He would help lift her spirits. He always could. Lord knows he had many times over the past few years while she mooned over losing Thorn. He was always there to make her laugh, smile, and improve her spirits.

"Oh, Zane, how wonderful to see you. I have missed you."

"Not much, it seems. I have heard through the London grapevine that your one true love has replaced me. Please tell me it is not true, Ivy dear. I fear my heart has been breaking since I've heard the rumors," Zane asked, clutching his heart.

Ivy turned a deep shade of red. She nodded her head at Zane.

"Yes, Thorn and I are to be married."

"Oh, be still my heart."

"Stop teasing me, Zane. I know better. Your heart has yet to be broken by any woman. But I cannot wait for the day it does. I hope I can help you the same way you have helped me."

"All in the duty of friendship, my dear. So, how did he win over your heart? The last I heard you would never give it to him."

"It is a long story. What brings you to Thornhill?"

"I heard you were here, and I was hoping you could lead me to Charles. I have an urgent message from him, and I cannot locate him anywhere."

"He is missing. So much has happened. I don't even know where to begin."

Zane led Ivy over to the bench to sit. He grabbed the flower basket and set it near their feet. When he sat next to her, he grabbed her hands in his. He rubbed his thumb back and forth over her fingers, offering her comfort.

"Why don't you start at the beginning, Ivy. Tell me everything. I will see how I can help," Zane urged Ivy to confide in him.

Ivy told Zane everything that happened, from Captain Shears to how she ended up on Thorn's ship to her stay at Thornhill Manor. She kept out the personal moments with Thorn. Zane Maxwell had been her closest confidante for the last few years, and they had an understanding between them. He understood how much she loved Thorn, and she understood how much he loved to stay away from the debutantes. Many people thought he courted Ivy and waited for them to announce their betrothal. But it was all a cover to keep the gentlemen away from Ivy and the smothering mamas away from Zane. Zane liked to flirt with her, and it made Ivy feel attractive, but she knew he was never serious about her. She even flirted with him on occasion, not that he was hard to flirt with.

Zane was as attractive as Thorn, but in a wild way that set women on edge. He was tall and had dark hair, and he liked to wear all his suits in black. His mysterious air drove the entire ladies of the ton crazy. But it was his eyes that always drew them in. They were so dark and soulful. When he laid his eyes on a lady, they were hypnotized. They couldn't glance away from him even if they wanted to. Ivy watched many women try to discover his secrets and fail. His raspy voice made their bodies tingle. Ivy listened to the women of the ton talk about how sexy his voice was when he whispered as he made love to them. She realized all she had to do was to give Zane a signal she was ready to move on from Thorn and he would court her. But she never did. Whoever captured Zane's heart would be a very lucky lady, indeed.

She told him how Thorn searched for Charles everywhere and could not find him. She confided everything to him, even about the conspiracy.

"I will help Thorn find Charles for you. Now, tell me what else is troubling you? I see the sadness in your eyes, my dear."

"It's Thorn. Ever since we returned to Thornhill Manor, he avoids me. It is like he doesn't want to be anywhere near me. I think he is having second thoughts. I love him so much, Zane. I don't think I can handle having him break my heart again." Ivy burst into tears.

Zane pulled Ivy into his arms and let her cry on his shoulder. This wasn't the first time he held Ivy as she cried over Thorn. He wanted to punch Thorn for the heartache he put Ivy though all these years. Then punch him again for her confusion now. Thorn didn't realize how lucky he was to have Ivy's love. Lord knew Zane tried to have it. But Ivy loved only one man and would only ever love one man, and that man was Marcus Thornhill.

Ivy thought Zane was just a friend. But in truth, Zane was a little in love with Ivy himself. Not the love Ivy needed. Just the selfish love that only Zane knew how to give. If she would have ever given him a hint she wanted more than friendship, he would have loved her with all his heart. At least as much as he was capable of.

"Ivy dear, how could he not love you? He is probably staying away because he can't keep his hands off you and doesn't want to compromise you."

Ivy blushed again, and Zane realized Thorn already compromised her. It must have happened on his ship. The lucky bastard. Thorn didn't recognize the gift of Ivy, but Zane would make him realize it. He would help Ivy one last time.

"I can tell that has already happened. Well then, we will have to make him jealous."

Ivy tried to refuse. That was not how she wanted to handle Thorn, but somebody cleared their throat and interrupted her. She looked to see Thorn in the garden and realized he saw her take comfort in Zane's arms. She rose and tried to rush to Thorn when Zane's hand ran slowly along her arm. He stood next to her as his hand lingered on her hand and gave it a light squeeze. Ivy glanced at Zane, and he gave her a nod as he dropped her hand. Ivy looked at Zane in confusion and then glanced away as she realized what he attempted to do.

Thorn did not miss the exchange between Ivy and Zane. He missed none of their interaction since Zane came into the rose garden. He'd wandered into her room, looking for her, and saw her out her bedroom window. He stared at her cutting roses like she had all those years ago when they shared their first kiss. He hoped for a private moment with her because he missed her like crazy these last two weeks. Thorn tried to stay away from her so she could make a full recovery, but it was harder than he thought. When she waited in his room at night, it took everything in his power to not lie her on his bed and make love to her. But instead he played the gentlemen, carried her to her own bed, tucked her in, and watched her while she slept. He needed to taste her lips under his. He could not concentrate on his search today as she kept sneaking into his thoughts. Thorn thought if he could spend a few moments with her and hold her, kiss her, then he would feel more refreshed for his search of Charles.

When he saw Zane pull Ivy into his arms and comfort her, he almost lost it. He never felt so jealous in his life. He tried to calm himself, but as he observed them together, it only made it worse. His mother tried to warn him about their friendship for all these years, but Thorn ignored the warnings. Zane was a friend and knew of his love for Ivy. He promised Thorn he would watch out for her while he was away. But after he saw them together, he was afraid Zane had fallen for Ivy too.

"Am I interrupting you two?" Thorn asked.

Ivy rushed over to Thorn quickly and grabbed his hands.

"No, Thorn. Zane has come to search for Charles. He is the agent we have been waiting for. I have filled him on everything that has happened. He said he will help you find Charles. Isn't this wonderful? You two can find Charles and end the treason together."

"Welcome back, Thorn." Zane reached to shake Thorn's hand.

Thorn shook Zane's hand and pulled Ivy against his side with his other arm.

"It is good to finally be home," he told Zane as he looked into Ivy's eyes.

When Ivy avoided his eyes, he pulled her closer to him and watched the blush spread across her cheeks at his display of affection in front of their friend. He knew he made it uncomfortable for her, but wanted Zane to understand Ivy was his and his alone. Also, he sent a silent message to Ivy that he would not share her with anybody else.

Zane laughed as he noticed his friend show his dominance. He realized Thorn was not indifferent to Ivy. He only needed a little guidance in the right direction. He would have a little fun as he showed Thorn how desirable Ivy was to every man.

"Will you stay for lunch, Zane?" Ivy asked.

"Yes, my lady. I will."

Ivy laughed as she bent to gather her basket of roses. Thorn missed her laugh and was jealous it wasn't directed toward him. She walked away from them before he could stop her.

"I will have cook set another plate for lunch," Ivy spoke over her shoulder as she walked inside.

Thorn watched Ivy leave and clutched his fists in frustration. He wanted a moment alone with her but was now stuck alone with Maxwell. When he looked at Zane, he found him laughing at him, so he snarled back. He stalked away from Zane and knew his friend would follow. Thorn went to his father's study, where he poured Maxwell and himself a drink. He handed the whiskey to Zane, who made himself comfortable on the couch.

"I hear congratulations are in order, my friend," Zane said, lifting his glass for a toast.

Thorn nodded his head and drank the whiskey in one gulp. He went back, refilled his glass, and settled in a chair. Thorn waited for Maxwell to speak, knowing it wouldn't take long. He proved himself correct when Maxwell questioned Thorn on Charles's disappearance.

"Have you had any success in finding him? Do you have any clue where he might have gone?"

"No, and the longer he is gone the more I fear for his life—and for Ivy's."

"Why do you fear for Ivy's life?"

"Because Captain Shears wants her dead. I have not informed Ivy of this threat. So far, she has stayed close to the house, so I have not had to worry. But I know she grows restless and wants to help. I am pleased you are here; you can help me go through Charles's papers and help me understand them. They make no sense. Also, you can help me keep an eye on Ivy and keep her out of trouble. Can you stay with us?"

"I have taken a room at the Margate Inn. It will be the best way for me to discover more information. When you need me, send word as discreetly as possible and I will come help."

"Agreed. We had better join them for luncheon before we get in trouble."

"Oh, my friend, I think you are already in very deep trouble," Zane laughed as he followed Thorn.

As they ate luncheon, Zane charmed his mother and Ivy with his delightful stories of the ton. He filled them in with the latest gossip. Katherine and Ivy told them how the ball and wedding plans were coming along. Both women blushed and giggled at every word that came out of Maxwell's mouth. Thorn had enough. He wasted valuable time listening to Zane's stories. He had a best friend to find and a treason plot to stop, and it frustrated him to see Ivy fawning over Maxwell.

Thorn pushed back his chair and stood from the table. "If you have finished eating, Maxwell, we need to start on those papers," he growled.

"Of course, old man." Zane winked at both ladies as he stood to join Thorn.

"It has been a delight eating luncheon with you two gracious ladies. Thank you for the delicious meal." Zane bowed to the women.

"You are welcome, sir. It has been our pleasure." Katherine giggled.

"Thank you for staying to eat with us, Zane. I hope you can help Thorn. Also, thank you for helping in our search for Charles," Ivy said.

"I will do what I can, my dear." Zane reached for Ivy's hand and pressed a kiss to the back of it.

Thorn watched Zane kiss the back of Ivy's hand and gritted his teeth. His lips seemed to linger on her fingers a little too long. He wanted to snatch her hand out of his, but he didn't want to create a scene. He couldn't afford to offend Maxwell. He needed his help. But it didn't mean he had to enjoy watching them together. He would make sure they were never left alone together, and he would seek his mother's help with that. He would keep Maxwell busy with Charles's papers.

Maxwell walked from the dining room, and Thorn stood, looking at Ivy. She stared back at him as she waited for him to speak. He didn't know how to respond to her. Since he did not want his jealousy to show, he decided not to say anything at all. He nodded his head at her and followed Maxwell along the hall.

All he did was nod at her. He didn't speak to her all throughout the luncheon. What was the nod about? Couldn't he say anything to her? She didn't understand him at all. Ivy was glad Zane was there. She needed a friend now more than ever. She held so many doubts, and now she had even more. What was she supposed to think about Thorn's behavior? Zane gave her more attention in the last couple of hours than Thorn gave her since they left his ship. She couldn't ask Katherine about her fears. She would just reassure her Thorn was busy in his search for Charles. She would wait until she was alone with Zane again and talk to him more. Maybe he could learn more about what troubled Thorn while they worked together.

~~~~~~

Thorn and Maxwell poured over Charles's documents late into the night. They skipped dinner and ate sandwiches in the study. Charles's notes were in a secret code that only he could understand. They did not make any progress. George and Hamilton joined them and discussed what they learned in the neighboring towns.

"From what we gathered, the attacks will occur from Brighton to Margate. All the towns along the coast have evidence of Shears and his crew in their ports," Hamilton explained.

"There has been no sign of Charles either," George told them.

"Maxwell and I have had no luck trying to understand Charles's papers," Thorn said.

"Were there indications on what days the attacks will happen?" Maxwell asked.

"That was the strange part. Nobody knows of a definite date, only the rumors they heard. But we had a sense it would be soon. Has your crew had any luck following Shears?" George asked.

"No, he docked his ship in Hastings with no movement on his ship or with his crew. He still has a few of his crew watching your place. There have been no sightings of him near here, but I wouldn't put it past him to try soon. He will not leave Ivy alone much longer. That is why we need to locate Charles and stop Shears before it is too late."

"I will say goodnight gentlemen and return to the inn. I will see what I can uncover in town and check in with you tomorrow, Thorn," Zane said as he walked toward the door.

They told Maxwell goodnight as they followed him out of the study into the foyer. George and Hamilton continued to their bedrooms as Thorn walked Maxwell to the door. As they waited for the groom to bring his horse, Ivy came down the stairs. She walked over to Zane and rested her hand on his arm.

"Thank you, so much for your help, Zane. I will be forever indebted to you if you can help us find Charles."

Zane lifted Ivy's hand from his coat and brought it to his lips. He gently placed a kiss on the back of her hand as he let his lips linger longer than necessary. He winked at her as he lowered her hand back down.

"Anything for a dear friend. I bid you goodnight, my lady, and I shall visit with you more tomorrow."

Zane turned toward Thorn and saw the anger in his eyes. Zane smiled and slapped him on the back as he left. He started to whistle as he climbed on his horse. This would be fun; a little competition would keep Thorn on guard. It would make him appreciate Ivy even more. Then he would learn not to leave a beautiful lady alone for so many years. Friends or not, Ivy deserved so much more, and Zane would make sure she received her happy ending.

Thorn slammed the door behind Maxwell as he left. He then turned and leaned against the door as he regarded Ivy through hooded eyes. She raised her head and lifted her chin, as if she was innocent of any wrongdoing.

"You two seem awfully chummy, like a couple of bosom friends," Thorn commented.

"Yes, we are friends."

"It seems to be more than friendship, Ivy."

"I don't understand what you are talking about."

"Don't you? How would you explain what I saw in the garden earlier? That wasn't the kiss of a friend on your hand when he left. It was more of a lover's kiss."

"Are you trying to imply Zane and I are lovers? I think you would know for a fact that's not true."

"I am saying your friendship seems a little too close."

"Just because I have accepted your proposal does not mean I shall rid myself of past friendships. Zane is a friend who has been there for me, which is more than I can say for you."

"Is it more than friendship, Ivy?"

"Are you jealous, Thorn?"

Thorn ran his fingers through his hair in frustration. He didn't want to fight with Ivy. The truth was he was extremely jealous. Maxwell got to touch her today more than he had in the last two weeks. All he wanted to do now was to pull her into his arms and kiss her. He didn't want to wonder of a relationship between his own fiancée and friend. He realized he acted as a fool. His Ivy was too innocent to cheat on him. It was her nature to be open and sweet to everybody. He also realized Maxwell baited him and took pleasure from it. He never felt so frustrated in his life. Thorn must backtrack here, so he decided to start over. They were alone, and he didn't know for how much longer. So, why did he try to ruin their time together with an argument?

It actually worked. Zane's attempt at jealousy worked. Thorn is jealous of Zane. Ivy laughed to herself. Ivy watched as Thorn tried to get his emotions under control. He looked so sexy when he ran his fingers through his hair and when he acted like he didn't know what to do with himself. Why wouldn't he take her in his arms and kiss her? Ivy craved for his mouth to be on hers. She ached for his touch. She wanted to show any sign of his love for her, and he wanted to be with her. Zane told her she needed to make the first move. Ivy felt shy about being forward with Thorn but knew she had to try.

Ivy walked over to Thorn and laid her hand on his chest. She looked into his smoky dark eyes as she ran her hand up and down his chest over the buttons of his shirt. She nervously licked her lips and watched his eyes darken even more. Ivy reached with her hand to brush the lock of hair off his forehead to the side. As she slid her hand behind his neck, she stood on her tiptoes and brought her lips closer to his.

She slid her lips along his slowly, brushing them gently across his lips. He moaned against her mouth. Ivy slid her tongue across his lips as she guided her tongue inside his mouth. She tasted the whiskey he had drunk earlier. Her tongue explored the power she felt as she took control of their kiss. She let him know of her desire as her tongue danced along his. What Ivy couldn't say to Thorn she showed him with her kiss. He released a groan against her lips and tried to take over the kiss, but Ivy pulled away. She placed a soft kiss against his mouth and stepped away from him.

"Good night, Marcus," she whispered.

She turned and began her climb up the stairs. When she glanced over her shoulder, she saw the look of shock and arousal on Marcus's face. She smiled sweetly at him. He started toward her, but Ivy kept walking up the stairs.

"Ivy?"

"Sweet dreams, Marcus," Ivy replied as she continued to her room.

Marcus brought his fingers to his lips. He stood in awe of the kiss Ivy gave him—an amazing kiss that proved what an idiot he was. She'd made her point of what a jackass he was. He would dream tonight, but after a kiss like that, they wouldn't be of the sweet variety.

Chapter Eighteen

SAMMY SETTLED INTO HIS seat at the bar as he talked with the crew when he saw Earl Zane Maxwell come into the inn. The earl climbed the stairs as he passed the bar. A few moments later, Captain Shears climbed the same stairs. Sammy nodded at his men at what he witnessed.

"If I don't come back down within ten minutes, send a message to the capt'n on what we saw. I will see what I can find out," he gave instructions to the crew.

Sammy rushed up the back stairs and wandered along the hallway as he stayed in the shadows. He put his ear to each door as he tried to locate the room the earl was in. He wondered what the connection was between the two.

~~~~~

Zane closed the door to his room at the inn, only to have it thrust opened as Captain Shears sauntered in. The captain sat in the chair by the fire. Zane opened the door and looked along the hallway to make sure nobody noticed the captain had come into his room. When he realized the coast was clear, he shut the door again and turned toward the captain with a scowl on his face.

"What are you doing here, Shears?"

"My men have informed me you have visited our good friend, Captain Thornhill. I have come to learn what information you have discovered. Have they located Mallory yet?"

"I have no information for you, and I never will."

"But we had a deal, Maxwell."

"When you kidnapped Ivy Mallory, all deals became void. If you go anywhere near her again, I will destroy all that you have achieved."

"Well, well, it seems Lady Ivy has quite the fan club. Has she shared her favors with you too?" Shears asked.

Zane advanced on Shears, grabbing him by his overcoat and pulling him out of the chair. He swung his arm back and around to connect his fist with Shears's face. The captain never saw it coming.

"You will never speak of her again. Do I make myself clear, Captain?" Zane asked as he punched Shears in the gut. He dropped him before he stomped across the room. The captain struggled back to his feet as he clutched his stomach.

"You are double-crossing the wrong man," Shears told Maxwell.

"Is that a threat, Captain?"

"No, my lord, that is a promise. Also, you will hold your end of the bargain or else the great Captain Thornhill and his lovely Lady Ivy will pay with their lives." Shears did not wait for a reply from Maxwell as he threw open the door and stomped from the room.

Maxwell poured himself a drink as he dunked his hand into the cold water left out for him. He would have to ask the innkeeper for some fresh water to clean with later. He had gotten himself into quite a mess. Maxwell needed to solve his problems quickly before any more harm came to his friends. But first he must find Mallory before anyone else. Mallory held the answers and would know how to stop Shears. But where was he?

~~~~~~

Sammy pressed himself back into the darkened corner as the door opened to the earl's room. Shears stormed past him in anger as he wiped the blood from his face. Sammy listened to their argument outside the room but was unable to hear much of what they said. He needed to get word to the captain and let him know of this latest development.

When he returned downstairs to the taproom, he told the crew to keep an eye on Lord Maxwell. They were to report any activity to him. Sammy informed them he would ride to Thornhill Manor to let the captain know of the events that took place. When he arrived at the manor, the house was closed for the night, so he made himself a bed in the stables. He would talk to the captain in the morning with his report.

When Thorn arrived downstairs in the morning, he was told of Sammy's arrival by the butler.

"Send him into my father's study, Cleaves, and bring us coffee," Thorn ordered.

"Yes, my lord."

Thorn waited in the study for Sammy to join him. It must be important information for him to make the rough journey to the manor. Thorn understood how painful it was for Sammy to ride from the injury to his leg. The guilt plagued Thorn as he thought of how Sammy received his injury. He couldn't ask for a more loyal servant—or friend.

Sammy limped into the study to the chair in front of the desk where Thorn sat. He eased himself into the chair as he stretched his leg forward. He reached down to rub the sore muscles. His rest in the cool night air hadn't helped the ache in his leg any.

"It must be very important news for you to cause yourself such discomfort," Thorn noted.

"Yes, Captain, real important. I trust nobody else with the delivery of this news."

Sammy stopped talking as Cleaves came into the room with a tray of coffee and scones. He sat the tray on the desk and served them. He stepped back to give them some privacy.

"That will be all, Cleaves."

"Yes, my lord," Cleaves said as he bowed to Thorn. After he left the room, Thorn nodded his head for Sammy to continue.

"Well, last night me and the boys were having a drink at the Margate Inn. As we were there, I noticed Lord Maxwell come in and go upstairs to the rooms above."

"Yes, he is staying there. He will aide us with our search for Charles and to stop the treason. I don't understand how that has warranted a ride out here, Sammy."

"Well, Capt'n, he had himself a visitor I think you might be interested in," Sammy explained.

Thorn immediately thought of Ivy. She wouldn't have risked her life and reputation to sneak away to visit Maxwell, would she? Was there more to their friendship than she defended? After the kiss she gave them before she went to bed, Thorn wouldn't have thought so. But maybe there was more to the relationship than Thorn realized. After Sammy left, Thorn would find Ivy and tell her not to risk her life for Maxwell. He would deal with his hurt and her betrayal later. The most important thing was to keep Ivy keep safe from Shears and his crew. He understood how she felt confined with her stay at Thornhill, but it was for own best interest.

"We will keep it between us Sammy. I will have a talk with Ivy later today. This shouldn't happen again."

"Lady Ivy? What does she have to do with the earl?" Sammy asked, confused.

"She wasn't the visitor?" Obviously, they were talking of two different people.

"No, it was Captain Shears. That is what I've been trying to explain to you."

An immediate sense of relief filled Thorn. He also felt guilt. Why did he think his sweet Ivy would betray him? She wouldn't. His jealousy of their friendship made him insecure. He was the one who encouraged the friendship, and now their friendship turned him into a jealous monster. He needed to control his emotions for Ivy before he made accusations against the woman he loved. She did not deserve this from him.

"What was Shears doing in Maxwell's room?"

"I'm not for sure, Captain. I could not overhear much of anything. They were arguing, and when Shears left the room, he wiped blood from his face and clutched his side. But I heard Shears say something about a bargain with Maxwell."

"What kind of bargain?"

"I don't know, Captain. I left the crew watching him. They are to report his activity to me."

"Why don't you finish your breakfast and then we will take the carriage into town to learn what we can find out. We will give your leg a rest. Thank you for getting me this information."

"You're welcome, Captain. Your cook here always did make the best scones around."

"I wouldn't let Anton hear you saying that."

"That Frenchie? I'm not scared of him."

Thorn laughed as he leaned back in his chair. As Sammy rattled on about how delicious the scones were, Thorn gathered his thoughts together about Maxwell. What kind of bargain did he have with Captain Shears? Did it involve Ivy? He would keep an eye on him for a spell and attempt to draw it out of him. From here on, he would never leave Ivy alone in his company. He didn't trust Maxwell any more now than ever.

Thorn climbed the back staircase of the Margate Inn. He talked to his crew, and they hadn't seen Maxwell leave this morning. Thorn hoped to catch him off guard or in the act of meeting with Shears. He pressed his ear against the door but could not hear any activity inside the room. He knocked on the door, but Maxwell didn't open. A chambermaid walked by and shyly ducked her head when he noticed her looking at him. She bobbed a curtsy as she walked by him. Thorn would persuade her to let him inside the room.

"Miss, I was wondering if you could help me with something," Thorn asked the chambermaid.

"Yes, my lord. How may I be of service?"

"Well my good friend Lord Maxwell forgot something in his room and asked if I could bring it to him. Is there any way you can let me into his room?"

"Yes, my lord."

The chambermaid unlocked the door for Thorn and pushed the door wide for him. Thorn reached into his pocket, drew out a few coins, and laid them into the young girl's hand. He closed her hand and gently pressed his hand with hers.

"Thank you for your help miss. We can keep my being here a secret between us, can't we?" Thorn smiled at the maid.

The maid blushed at the touch of Thorn's hand on hers. She nodded her head, speechless from his attention. She bobbed a curtsy and quickly left the room.

After the maid left, Thorn pulled the door closed behind him. He wandered around the room looking for any clues of Maxwell's involvement with Shears. Obviously, his crew did not keep a very close eye on him since Maxwell was nowhere in the room. He would address his crew about being more diligent later. Thorn found Maxwell's baggage, searched through it, and only found clothes. He threw the bag down in disgust since he came up empty-handed when a secret compartment opened at the bottom. Thorn bent over, slid it open all the way, and pulled out some papers. As he scanned the documents, he realized they were in written in a secret code similar to those of Charles's papers. When they read through the papers the night before, Maxwell claimed ignorance at what they looked at. Thorn stayed up late in the night and was able to crack some of the code. From what Thorn could tell, these looked like shipments and the dates they were received. They also had coordinates of the hidden locations. If he was correct, this information lined up with what his and Ivy's father had learned.

As he slid the papers back into their hiding place, his hand scraped against another piece of paper. He unfolded the paper to find a drawing. It wasn't any drawing; it was a picture of Ivy. She sat on a blanket as she laughed at ducks waddling by. Thorn smiled and traced his fingers over the drawing as if he touched her. He wanted to take the drawing but didn't want Maxwell to realize he searched through his belongings. Thorn knew it was Maxwell who had drawn Ivy. The picture gave the detail of a man smitten with the young lady. Was Maxwell in love with Ivy? He wanted to crumple the paper and throw it in the fire. Then he wanted to find Maxwell and punch him in the face. But who could blame him? It was his fault Maxwell and Ivy were close. He was the one who left her and asked his friend to take care of her. Now, he was the one who must deal with jealousy whenever he saw them together.

Thorn heard a commotion outside the door, a loud thump, and water splashing.

"Oh, I am sorry, my lord. I am so clumsy; it slipped from my hands. I will repair your clothes for you, my lord."

"That's certainly all right, my darling. Accidents happen. Would you like to join me in my chambers and help me out of my wet clothes?" Maxwell said.

Thorn realized the chambermaid tried to warn him of Maxwell's return. He shoved the drawing and papers back into the secret compartment and settled the baggage back where he found it. He would have to compensate the chambermaid a few extra coins for her warning. Probably more than a few just for dealing with Maxwell's flirtation.

"No, sir, I cannot do that. I must get this mess cleaned before the landlord sees."

"Perhaps another time, my dear," Maxwell laughed as he opened his door and came into the room.

As he came through the door, he noticed Thorn had made himself at home in the chair by the fire. Déjà vu from the night before flashed across his mind. Would he ever get any peace in his own room? He looked around to see if there was anything out of place. He saw his baggage was in the same place he left it earlier this morning. After he closed the door, he walked over to the other chair and sat down.

"To what do I owe this unexpected visit?" Maxwell asked.

"I was in town and thought we could talk more on Charles's disappearance. Do you think there is a connection to Shears?"

"Is that all you wanted to visit about? Or is there another subject you wish to discuss?"

"What other subject would we have to discuss?" Thorn asked.

"Ivy."

"Ivy is none of your concern anymore."

"Well, at one time you made her my concern."

"You are no longer needed. I will take care of Ivy from here on out."

"There is one small problem with that, my friend."

"What problem would that be?"

"While you were away, Ivy and I have … shall we say, bonded quite closely as friends?"

Maxwell watched as Thorn tightened his fist against the arm of the chair. The angrier Thorn got, the more Maxwell decided to goad him. He hoped Thorn would show his true feelings for Ivy, so he could reassure her that Thorn loved her. Maxwell could see how jealous Thorn became. He decided to make him more jealous. He rose from his chair and walked across the room to pour them a couple of drinks.

"You see, we have spent many days and evenings together. I would take her for picnics and escort her to balls. We would take rides through Hyde Park and waltz among the ton. Over the course of time we would confide in each other our deepest wants and desires. So, you see, I shall always care for Ivy and she will for me." Maxwell handed Thorn his glass.

Thorn swiped the glass out of Maxwell's hand angrily and drank the fiery liquid in one gulp. It burned as it went down like the anger burned in his gut at Maxwell's words. If what Maxwell spoke was true and the picture proved his feelings for Ivy, then Thorn had competition for Ivy's affection. She said she loved him, but did she love Maxwell more? Could he give her up if Maxwell was who she wanted to be with? No, it was he who Ivy loved and desired more than anybody. She wouldn't kiss him and let him love her like he had if she wanted Maxwell.

"Do you love her?" Thorn gritted his teeth. He tried to keep his anger in check. He didn't want to tip Maxwell to the real reason he was there. But he needed this issue resolved now.

"Love. Such a funny word, don't you think, my friend?" Maxwell asked as he lowered himself back in the chair. He raised the glass to his lips and took a sip. Maxwell nursed his drink. He wanted to enjoy the smooth flavor coating his throat as he drank. To abuse such a fine liquid like Thorn did was a crime.

"No, it is a simple word, my friend," Thorn answered with sarcasm.

Maxwell laughed as he watched Thorn hold himself together. "How would you define love?"

"Love is the connection with another soul where you feel that you're dead without them. Love is wanting to be with them for the rest of their lives through all the good and bad. Love is your heart full and content when they hold it their hands," Thorn explained.

"Do you love Ivy?" Maxwell asked.

"With every last breath in my body I love her. Do you?"

"Yes."

"Does she feel the same way about you?" Thorn asked, even though he did not want to know the answer.

"Yes, I believe she does."

Thorn didn't know how to react. He sat in the chair and felt like he had been sucker-punched. He should have known Maxwell would fall in love with her. Who wouldn't? She was everything a man wanted. Obviously, with him away, Ivy placed her affections with somebody who was there for her. The irony of it was, he was the one who placed Maxwell in her life. He only had himself to blame for this. He needed to think. He had to leave this room. The walls were closing in on him. All he wanted to do was fight Maxwell for Ivy. But Ivy deserved so much more. He did not want to let her go, but he could not keep her if another held her heart.

Maxwell watched his friend struggle across from him. He should put him out of his misery and tell him the love he held for Ivy was only friendship. She had been there for him just as much as he had been there for her. She held his darkest secret and didn't judge him for it but guarded it as if it was her own. They formed a bond that no one could break apart. He knew Ivy felt the same way. He would make Thorn earn his love for Ivy. It was what Ivy deserved.

Thorn rose from his chair and walked out of the room, not uttering a word. He did not get the answers he wanted when he came to Maxwell's room. But he left with answers and more questions he needed to ask of himself or Ivy. He passed Sammy and his crew in the taproom without a word and climbed into his carriage. As the carriage returned to Thornhill Manor, Thorn leaned against the cushions and closed his eyes.

Exhaustion seeped into Thorn's body. He couldn't seem to find Charles, the treason plot was closer to happening any day now, and now he wasn't sure of Ivy's love. Thorn ran his hand down over his face and covered his mouth as he released a huge sigh. What would he do about any of this mess?

He needed to get away and think. There was one more place he wanted to search for Charles. It was a secret hiding place they escaped to as children. It was a place they would hide to escape the pressure of learning to follow in their fathers' footsteps. They both were groomed to be future dukes and all that it entailed. For young boys, the pressure overwhelmed them. He would go there today to look and stay awhile. It always brought him peace when he was younger. He would ride there and solve his problems. It would also save him from running into Ivy on the estate. He needed to control his emotions and decide what was best for her before he saw her again. He didn't know what he would do if he saw her, knowing what he did about the love she had for Maxwell. Thorn experienced anger and sorrow at the whole situation. He didn't want her to see, and he didn't want to take his frustration out on her. She had been through too much already, and she deserved so much greater.

Chapter Nineteen

IVY HEARD THE POUNDING of the horse's hooves as the carriage headed to the stable. She rose from the couch where she read a book in the library and strolled to the windows. She hoped to catch a glimpse of Thorn. Thorn alighted from the carriage and shouted instructions to Peter, the stable boy. Peter ran to the house as Thorn walked into the stables. Ivy sat at the large bay windows and waited for Thorn to exit the stables to come into the house. She waited for him all morning. When she went to his room after he wasn't at breakfast, his valet told her Thorn rode into Margate with Sammy on business. Ivy then settled in the library to wait. It was the perfect place to spot Thorn when he returned home. As soon as he came into the house Ivy would try to steal a few moments alone with him. Maybe they could continue where they left off last night.

It was such a sweet kiss they shared. Ivy didn't know what she enjoyed more; taking the initiative with the kiss or the shock on Thorn's face when she kissed him. She smiled to herself. She would never forget the look on his face. She wished he would hurry and come into the house before Katherine found her and wanted to discuss more wedding plans.

Peter emerged from the house with a bag slung over his shoulder. He entered the stable with the bag and disappeared from her view at the window. Ivy wondered what Peter grabbed from the house and if it was for

Thorn. Peter led Pirate from the stables and attached the bag to the horse. He also tucked a blanket inside the bag. What was this for? Where was Thorn going? Wasn't he even going to come inside and say goodbye? When Thorn emerged from the stables, he had changed into his captain's gear. He discarded his waistcoat and trousers for a flowing captain's shirt and breeches. He jumped onto his horse and said a few words to Peter. Peter nodded his head at Thorn. Thorn took off across the lawn. After he had gotten a short distance from the house he stopped and turned. It appeared he stared at her though the library windows, like he knew she watched him. He ran his hand through his hair and turned back in his saddle and galloped away. Ivy lifted her hand to the window to wave at him, but he already left.

"Where are you going?" Ivy whispered.

"He said he needed to get away to think," a voice said from behind her.

Ivy turned and was startled to find Hamilton regarding her from the fireplace. She thought she was alone in the library. She was embarrassed to have been caught watching for Thorn and talking to herself.

"What does he need to think about?" Ivy asked.

"He didn't say, my dear. But something troubles him deeply, more than Charles and the treason."

"Did he tell you what it was and where he would go?"

"No, but he only goes to one place to think."

"The secret cave?" Ivy guessed.

"Yes, now the question is, are you going to let him think alone?" Hamilton asked.

"He doesn't want to see or talk to me. I have tried many times these past weeks. It is like he avoids me."

"Well, now is your perfect chance to get him to talk to you. He won't have anywhere to run away to."

"Katherine will not let me ride after him."

"You leave Katherine to me, honey. I will keep her occupied elsewhere while you ride to Thorn. I owe you this."

"I don't understand."

"Years ago, I told Thorn to leave you alone. I felt you were too young for him, and he still had too many wild oats to sow. I didn't want you to wait for word that he might never come home. You were young and needed to enjoy the things he had already enjoyed. I realize now I was wrong to separate you two. You two could have enjoyed these last few years together instead of apart. It was wrong of me to make you wait for the right moment. Because in life there is no right time, only the time there is to enjoy. I know my son loves you with all his heart. What I don't understand is why he still tries to hold back his love from you. Your mission is to ride after him and learn why. I will have Peter saddle Mercury for you. Go change into something warm; it might be a few hours before you can return. Once you reach Thorn, I will give instructions for Peter to return to the stables."

Ivy listened to what Hamilton told her and understood why Thorn left her all those years ago. Hamilton only held her best interest at heart, like a father would. She noticed how Hamilton regretted what he did and how he now tried to make amends. Ivy went him and grabbed his hands to hold them between hers.

"Thank you, Father."

Hamilton laughed in relief and pulled Ivy into his arms for a hug. "Now wear a cloak to cover your hair. We don't want anybody to realize you are leaving the grounds. Now hurry before it gets dark and Katherine finds you before you can leave."

Ivy rose on her tiptoes, kissed his cheek, and ran from the room. She headed to her room and changed her clothes quickly. She brushed her hair back and tied it with a green ribbon. Ivy pulled out her dark black cloak and wrapped herself it in before she left her room. As she started her descent on the staircase, she heard Katherine ask Mabel if she had seen Ivy. They searched the rooms for her and asked the servants if they had seen Ivy lately. Ivy watched Hamilton come into the foyer and spin a story to Katherine about how he saw her in the gardens because she wanted to be alone. He told Katherine to leave her be for a while and started whispering to Katherine. Ivy listened to Katherine giggle at Hamilton and knew she could sneak away.

Ivy snuck outside to the stables. Peter had Mercury saddled and ready to go for her. He helped her mount the horse, then settled in behind her with his own horse, and they kicked their horses into a sprint after Thorn. Ivy raced her horse faster because she wanted to reach Thorn before nightfall. Before they reached the cave, Ivy slowed her horse to a stop. She motioned for Peter to help her down. Peter helped Ivy from her horse and they walked the horses the remaining way. Ivy did not want to alert Thorn of their presence until Peter was on his way back to the house. If Thorn saw Peter, he would order Peter to take Ivy back with him. She tied Mercury next to Pirate and whispered in their ears to keep quiet.

"Thank you, Peter for your help. You can return now," Ivy whispered.

"Please be careful, my lady."

"I will."

Peter walked his horse back, climbed in the saddle, and rode away. She wandered to the cave and looked inside. Thorn was nowhere to be seen. She looked along the cove and saw him walking in the sand. He walked along, stopping every now and then and picking up rocks. He would throw the rocks out into the sea and watch as they skipped along the surface. Thorn looked lost. Ivy wanted to go down to him and wrap him in her arms to help him find his way. It was if he scented her presence, for his gaze rose and their eyes met.

Chapter Twenty

MARCUS LOOKED UP AND saw his thoughts appear at the entrance of the cave. Her hair came loose and billowed in the wind that came off the sea. She pulled her hair away from her face as she watched him, waiting for his reaction to her appearance. He paused as he gazed at her. She was everything to him and more. He could no more live without her than he could not draw another breath into his body. He took off at a run and climbed the cliff to the cave in a hurry to reach her. When he reached the entrance, he brushed her hair back from her face and swept her into his arms. Marcus lowered his head to kiss her deeply, drawing the very breath out of her and into himself. He carried her over to the blanket and lowered her body to slide along his.

As he broke the kiss, he leaned his forehead against hers and breathed deeply. Marcus gathered Ivy deep into his arms as he held her tightly, but gently, against him. He was afraid to let her go, afraid he imagined her in his arms, and afraid their kiss wasn't real. Afraid she was here to tell him how she felt about Maxwell. He wasn't ready to let her go. He wanted one last time with her to be his. Marcus needed her like never before. He would be a selfish bastard and take her one more time. Then he would let her go. Marcus knew it wasn't fair to her, but he was past caring at this point.

Ivy stared at the anguish passing across Marcus's face and wanted to comfort him. She reached with her hand and rested it along his cheek. He turned his head and placed a gentle kiss into her palm.

"Marcus?"

Marcus pressed his fingers against her lips and shook his head no. He didn't want there to be any words between them. He just wanted her. Wanted to taste her, touch her, and make love to her. He wanted to leave his mark on her to feel for the rest of her life. Wanted to make sure she never forgot him and how he made her feel, even though she loved another.

He slid her cloak off her shoulders and let it drop to the cave floor. Marcus made quick work of the buttons on the back of her dress and slid it off her body. Ivy lay before him in her chemise. It was made of a delicate lace, so delicate it hardly covered her body. It was transparent. He could make out her nipples pressed against the lace. They were hard for him. He slid his thumbs across them. He rubbed his thumb back and forth across the lace and heard Ivy moan. Marcus saw how Ivy's eyes darkened with desire as he touched her.

He continued to watch her reaction as he slid the straps down her shoulders and the shift off her body. When he slid his palms to her breasts, he brushed her nipples before he took her breasts into his hands. He softly squeezed them as he gently pinched her nipples. After he heard Ivy's quick intake of breath, he lowered his lips and took her nipple into his mouth. His tongue stroked it back and forth as his teeth grazed the tip. Ivy swayed into his arms as he bent her back a little, so he could make love to her breasts. He teased them with his tongue and lips. His actions made her fingers slide through his hair as she pulled his head closer. Her fingers tightened as she grasped at his hair.

Marcus moved his lips down lower, as he placed soft kisses along her stomach and moved lower. He kissed his way to the garter that held her tights to her lovely long legs. He kissed the inside of her thigh, his tongue slowly stroking up higher, then back down again. When he moved to other thigh, he repeated his action, but this time he paused at the heat of her body. He felt the heat rise off her and the smell of her ready for him. Softly he blew a whisper of breath at her core.

She tightened her grip on his shoulders, and he heard her moan his name. He saw a drop of dew nestled in her curls and knew she was wet for him, ready to take her and make her his. He was not going to rush any of this; he would make her melt for him. Marcus wanted to make every minute last for as long as he could. He wanted to savor her and this moment to make it last a lifetime in memories, because there would be no other for him. Ivy was his heart and soul and he would never give it away to another woman in his lifetime.

Marcus ran his hand along her leg and lifted it over his shoulder, opening her for him to see, touch, and taste. The open air along her thigh made her shiver in his arms. Was it the air or the anticipation of what was to come? He hoped it was the latter. When he ran his fingers over her garter, he slid her tights down her legs, his lips kissing a long trail in their wake. He began the path of kisses back up her legs again until he reached the top of her leg. His tongue slid along the crease at the edge of her womanhood. His tongue stroked back and forth, teasing her, making her body ache for his mouth on her wetness. He lowered her leg off his shoulder and listened to her moan of frustration. He smiled as he realized she became frustrated at his teasing. But she never said a word. She understood he didn't want to talk. Maybe she wanted this goodbye as much as he did, because this would be a goodbye. He could not hold her to him when she loved another. Marcus would have to let her go. He would not let her get caught in his thorns. She needed to grow wild and free. He would not cut her down to be snared by him.

He reached and pulled her closer to him. As she lowered her body next to him, Marcus ran his hands over her body. Not wanting to lose a moment in touching her, kissing her, loving her. When she reached his level, she ran her hands down to his shirt and pulled it over his head. Marcus caught his breath as her hands touched him. Her touched would undo him every time. When she pressed her lips against his chest, he wanted to press her to the cave floor and take her right at that moment. He didn't think it was possible, but he grew even harder. He had craved her touch these last few weeks more than he realized.

Ivy needed to touch Marcus so badly. She missed his touch, and she missed touching him. He made love to her like a desperate man. Like it would be the last time he would ever make love to her. Ivy didn't understand why, but she was too far gone in her desire to question him. There would be time later to understand. She craved his touch and kisses far past the point of understanding anything. Her fingers slid across his hard, smooth chest, then dipped and swayed across his muscles. She sensed his need as his body tightened under her touch. She needed to taste him, so she slid her lips across his chest. Her lips began to dip and nip across his muscles. She tasted the sea on his body as she ran her tongue along his neck tasting the salt of the sea that splashed on him. Ivy worked her way to his lips. Her tongue slid across his lips, licking hungrily. When he parted his lips for her, Ivy slid her tongue inside his mouth tasting him. She could feel Marcus holding back from taking control of the kiss. She knew he held onto a thin control by letting her play. She felt the tightness of his body against hers, ready to explode.

Ivy wanted to press the limits to more of his control. She wanted him to explode and love her like he did on his ship. As she kissed him deeper, her tongue stroked his, her hand lowered to the front of his trousers. She slid her hand across his hardness and teased him as he teased her. Her body ached below for his kiss and touch, but he denied her the need of him. She figured what was good for her was equally good for him. Her hand continued to tease him, lightly brushing back and forth across the placket of his trousers. He grew bigger from her light touch and felt the moan coming from deep in his chest through their kiss.

Ivy broke off the kiss and glanced to the front of his trousers, so she could see what her touch did to him. Her fingers trembled as she worked to undo the buttons of his trousers, slowly unbuttoning them. When she had them unbuttoned, she slid them over his buttocks. She watched as his cock sprang out of his pants and into her hands. Ivy moved her fingers over his cock as she touched the hard steel. Marcus was smooth to her touch, but hard as she gripped him around her fingers. She heard him groan, as if he was in pain. When Ivy raised her eyes to his, she saw the storm darken in his eyes to a midnight blue. The storm wasn't one of pain but of a desire Ivy had never seen before. This was unlike any desire they shared before. This was one of a man and a woman in the storm of a passion they could not deny. Overcome with passion from this storm, Ivy needed to show Marcus he could no longer deny the passion they were meant to have, now and forever.

Ivy lowered her head and took Marcus into her mouth. She slid her mouth over him, slowly tasting him. Her lips came back up just as slow. She slowly slid to the tip of his cock, her tongue slowly swirling around. As she brought him in between her lips, she began to softly suck on the tip. Marcus's hands ran though her hair as he held her head in his lap. She slid her mouth along his cock, her tongue softly stroking, as she took him deeper into her mouth. Marcus groaned her name louder as she took him in and out of her mouth. Her mouth made love to him like he had made love to her before. Ivy wanted to give him the same pleasure he gave her. She wanted him to lose control. She needed him to lose control. Ivy felt him harden in her mouth as she made love to him.

Marcus knew this was wrong. He should never allow Ivy to do this to him. She gave her heart to another man. This was another selfish act for him. But he could no more deny her touch and kiss than he could deny his love for her. He did not have the will to stop her. He needed and craved her love like a ship stuck in a storm craved the sun and soft gentle wind. That was what Ivy did to him. She made him feel like a ship fighting to stay upright in a storm. But when she kissed and touched him, she was his sun, and her touch was the soft gentle wind. He was ready to explode, but he did not want it to be this way. When he lost full control, he wanted to be inside her body and hold her in his arms as they both lost control together.

He pulled her into his arms and kissed her with all the passion inside his body. Their lips fused into one as they tasted each other. Marcus lay Ivy back on the blanket. He stood and removed the rest of his clothing as he gazed upon her body spread out before him. He lowered himself back down between her legs and removed her other stocking. When she lay naked before him, he stared and watched the beautiful blush spread across her body, wrapping it in a pink hue. He ran his hands along her legs and spread them open wider for him. His thumb brushed across her core, and he touched the wetness between her folds. Ivy opened her legs even wider after he touched her. It was as if she craved his touch as much as he craved to touch her.

He slid his fingers up and down in her wetness. His fingers dipped inside her, she tightened around his fingers as they slid in and out of her. Ivy arched her back, bringing her core higher so his fingers could slide in deeper. He slid his fingers in as deep as he could while his thumb stroked her clit back and forth. The dewy wetness glided over her hard clit. Her body became tight as a string ready to break. As he pulled his fingers away, she groaned in frustration. He slid his fingers to his mouth, tasting and licking her sweetness from his fingers as he watched her.

She raised her hips up off the cave floor, wanting and needing his touch on her again. Marcus licked his lips and brought his fingers to her lips. She licked and tasted herself on his fingers. When she flicked her tongue out to draw his thumb into her mouth to suck on it, Marcus groaned and pulled his thumb away. He lowered his head to her core, brought his hands underneath her buttocks and pulled her into his mouth as his mouth devoured her center. He drank from her like a man starved for a thirst only she could quench.

Marcus slid his tongue deep inside to taste every last drop her body had for him. Ivy exploded as he licked, kissed, and sucked at her. Marcus wouldn't stop. He knew Ivy had more for him. He wanted more from her. His tongue and fingers were everywhere, stroking nice and slow, then quicker as her body tightened under his tongue. He worked his tongue to her clit in slow strokes as his tongue pressed harder as his strokes became slower. He could feel the pressure building in her again as his fingers dipped and swayed, bringing her to her crest.

Ivy released a scream as she fell apart under Marcus's mouth. He tasted her explosion and the spasms of aftermath her body released under his touch. He slowly kissed his way along her body as his fingers continued to keep her fire alight, her heat continued to consume her as it did him. Her body became soft and relaxed under his, as it waited for them to become one with each other. His mouth stopped along the way at her breasts and he softly sucked them into his mouth and felt her nipples harden at the stroke of his tongue.

His mouth continued his journey upward and settled on her lips. He drank at the sweetness of her lips as he slid himself inside her. So slowly they could remember every slow stroke that joined their bodies as one. He watched her eyes grow wider at the joining of their bodies. Her hands glided over his body to hold onto him as he took them on a ride. He slid in and out of her body with long slow strokes. Her body tightened again around his cock. Marcus slid into her faster and harder as she came apart around him again. He slowed his rhythm again to build her wave, so he could crash down into her again.

Ivy felt her body crashing into Marcus's. She held onto to him like an anchor. The waves of pleasure that racked her body consumed her. She brought his head down for a kiss, kissing him deeply and hungrily wanting all he had to give her. She raised her hips to his and rode the waves of pleasure their bodies gave each other. She needed to touch him all over, and her hands glided everywhere across his body. Their waves climbed higher in their bodies as they crested at the highest peak. Marcus paused as their bodies were about to go over. They stared deep into each other's eyes for a moment of time as their bodies were suspended in air. Marcus slid himself deeper inside of her as they exploded into the waves, crashing their bodies back down into the gentle sway of the sea.

Marcus rolled over and brought Ivy into his arms and lay her across his chest. He stroked her hair in a calming way. Her body curled into his as she rested her palm across his stomach. She gently stroked her fingers back and forth. Her fingers stopped their caress, and Marcus knew she drifted to sleep. He continued to stroke her hair as she slept. He never even came close to this kind of passion in his life before and knew he never would again. Marcus felt complete.

Chapter Twenty-One

WHEN IVY AWOKE, SHE noticed Marcus had fallen asleep with her. The last thing she remembered before she drifted to sleep was Marcus stroking her hair. Ivy lay her head back on Marcus's chest and ran her fingers along his side. She found the scar she encountered earlier while they made love. She ran her finger across it, lightly tracing it from his side to his stomach and back again. Ivy bent her head and placed little kisses along the path of the scar. A tear slid down her face and landed on the scar.

"Ivy?"

Ivy looked at the questions in Marcus's eyes. She wanted to answer them, if only he would ask them instead of shutting her out. If he wouldn't ask her his questions, then it wouldn't stop her from asking her questions. This time he would answer them for her.

"What happened here, Marcus?" Ivy asked as her fingers continued to trace the scar.

Marcus tried to rise from the floor, sliding Ivy off him. But Ivy would not be pushed away any longer. She wrapped her hands around his waist to stop his movements. She didn't fight for him all those years, but she would fight for him now.

Marcus sighed and slid to lean against the cave wall. He would answer her questions, then he needed to return her to the house. She was not safe here with Shears's men crawling all over the place. He would give her the answers she sought and then let her go. He would keep her safe for Maxwell, if that was who she desired.

"My crew was ambushed along the coast of France. An agent who worked for both sides fed us false information. The other side offered him more money, so my crew and I were caught in the middle. The double agent informed the French the location of my ship and the cargo held onboard."

"What was on your ship?"

"Not what, but whom. We gave refuge to one of Napoleon's highest-ranking officers. He lost his wife and child at the hands of Napoleon's idiocy. He held top war secrets that he shared with us. In return, we gave him and his daughter a safe place to hide until the war was finished. But the other agent told the French of our plans for this officer and his daughter."

"The French invaded our ship in the dead of night. Most of my men were in the local village. We had been at sea for months, and they enjoyed a much-needed break. We disguised ourselves as a merchant ship so not to draw attention. When they attacked, they hit the men I had on guard. Sammy was one of those men. They beat him badly and crushed his leg with a barrel. When I heard the commotion, I hid the officer's daughter and ran on deck. By that time, they already captured the officer. As I charged at them, they slit his throat before I could reach him. I pulled out my sword and fought their leader."

"Another English ship at dock came to our rescue. The leader of the attack sent out the signal for them to retreat. They accomplished what they came for—to kill the officer. But they were unaware of his daughter hidden on the ship. I failed to keep him safe, but I would do everything in my power to protect his daughter."

"Did you protect her?"

"She protected herself, or so she thought."

"How did she do that?" Ivy inquired.

"She climbed to the upper deck of the ship after the fighting stopped. That was when she noticed her father dead. She thought I betrayed her father, so she took the knife stuck in his boot and charged at me. My crew saw her charging but were unable to stop her in time. She stabbed the knife into my side and dragged it across my stomach. I think it was her gut reaction to act out like she did. When she saw the blood and realized she caused it, she dropped the knife and backed away from me. I will never forget the horror written across her face. She lost everybody she loved and became violent in turn. I tried to reach her, but the cut was too deep, and I collapsed. I lost a lot of blood. She ran off the ship and escaped into the night."

"By the time I came to a few days later, she was nowhere to be found. I ordered my crew to search for her, but they came up empty-handed. We couldn't stay in port much longer without the French on our tail. Not being able to give her shelter has been one of my biggest regrets. I have sent inquiries among my contacts, but nobody has seen her."

"Is that how Sammy received his limp?"

"Yes, if it wasn't for me keeping the officer onboard without extra protection, he wouldn't have gotten injured like that."

"It isn't your fault, Marcus. Those are the consequences of war."

"But, Ivy, I let my guard down. It is the guilt I will have to live with for the rest of my life."

"I hope you will share your burden of guilt with me to help ease the burden you carry on your shoulders."

Marcus did not respond to Ivy. He needed to end this right now. It was torture dragging this out even though it helped to unburden his troubles with her. He felt a lightness in his heart he hadn't felt for a long time. But at the same time, there was the extreme heartache at the loss of her love.

"I will not burden you with my guilt, Ivy."

"Don't you understand? It is not a burden, but a joining of our love to make it more bearable for you to handle."

"But it isn't really our love, is there?"

"What are you talking about, Marcus?"

"I don't have your full love, do I? You love another."

Ivy stood and tugged the blanket around her body. She felt naked enough without having her emotions laid bare before him.

"And who am I to love other than you, Marcus Edward Thornhill?"

"Let us not play games with each other anymore, Ivy. I won't keep you from your true heart's desire. I realize now I am being selfish for tying you to me with our engagement. Also, I am even more guilty by making love to you. But I couldn't help myself. I have loved you for years, and I could no longer deny myself the pleasure of your body. I should not have taken your virginity; it was not mine to take. If I had known of your love for him, I would have fought the temptation of your body. We will find a way to break this engagement as soon as I know you are safe. I will plead your case to your father and smooth the way for you to marry your true love."

"Games? You are the one playing games. I have poured out my love to you in words and with my body. What more do you want from me? What other love? There has only ever been one love in my life. I will love him for all of eternity. But he is too stupid to realize it. If you do not want me, why have you teased me with your passion and these phony words? Do I not deserve better from you? I knew I should never have given you my heart again. But I could no more resist you than I could resist the love I feel for you."

Ivy gathered her clothes and moved deeper in the cave to get dressed. She couldn't stay with him any longer. She did not understand the games he played. He had nerve accusing her of playing games and loving somebody else. Who else was she supposed to have loved?

Ivy turned as she stomped back to Marcus. She dropped her clothes as she stood with her hands on her hips, her foot tapping on the cave floor in anger as she demanded more answers.

"Well, since I am to have given my heart to another man, would you be so kind to let me know the name of this mysterious gentleman?" Ivy asked.

Marcus listened to the sarcasm in Ivy's words. Why was she playing coy? He saw the picture in Maxwell's bag. The love she held for him was evident in the drawing. Maybe she didn't realize her affection for Maxwell was love. Marcus needed to explain the difference to her. She was very young and naïve, and maybe she didn't understand her true feelings. He would put his love and pride to the side for her happiness.

"Zane Maxwell," Marcus answered.

"Zane?"

"Yes, you love Maxwell."

Ivy laughed. She'd never heard anything in the world so hilarious. She doubled over laughing and sank to the ground. Marcus's jealousy of Zane had hit a new high. Or was it a new low? How on earth did he come to that conclusion? Ivy saw confusion cross over Marcus's face as she continued to lie on the ground laughing. It then turned to anger. It served him right that she laughed at him. Of all the idiotic things she ever heard, this one was priceless. If he thought she loved Zane, then why not play along for a few minutes?

"Oh, Marcus, what a relief you have guessed what I was unable to tell you."

"So, you do not deny your love for Maxwell?"

"No, I can no longer deny what my heart speaks to be true. I love Zane Maxwell."

"He has admitted the same to me as of this morning."

"He admitted to you that he loves me?"

"Yes."

"How else did you come to this conclusion?"

"I happened across a picture he drew of you kept hidden in a secret compartment of his bag."

"What picture is this?"

"A picture of you at the park watching ducks."

Ivy remembered the drawing. Zane wanted to sketch the afternoon Ivy tagged along with him to Hyde Park. Ivy confided in Zane her heartache of missing Thorn. Zane told her stories about the trouble they got into at school. Zane's stories about Thorn helped to ease the ache in her heart. He showed her the picture after he finished. It was a picture of a woman in love.

"Would you like for me to tell you about the love I have for Zane?"

Ivy watched as Thorn tightened his hands into fists at his sides. She really should quit teasing him, but he was the one who started this farce. Ivy came to her feet and walked over to stand in front of Thorn. She let the blanket drop off her shoulders but held it tight right in front of her breasts. Her breasts swelled out of the blanket, ready to be exposed. Ivy watched Thorn's eyes drop to her breasts and saw him swallow his comment. She relaxed her hand and let the blanket gape open for him to see more.

"Well Thorn, would you like me to explain the love I hold for Zane?" Ivy asked again.

Thorn was in agony. He did not want to hear about her love for another man while she stood in front of him wearing nothing but a blanket. She allowed the blanket to gape open for him to see her creamy skin hiding underneath. He wanted to reach out and caress her body with his hands. Then when he finished caressing her with his hands, he wanted to caress her body with his mouth. Thorn shook his head at his train of thought. She distracted him with her beautiful body. Did she even realize what she did to him? He needed to stop this now. He reached to close her blanket and dragged her close to his body.

"How can you speak about your love for another man when your actions tease me with your body? Do you even realize what you are doing, Ivy? I cannot control myself around you. You need to get dressed so I can return you to the house."

"I will not get dressed. I will not run from us anymore, Thorn."

"There is no us anymore, Ivy. You have spoken of your love for Zane. I will not stand in your way. I need a few days to straighten this out with our families."

"Just answer this for me, Thorn, and I will return to the house. Do you love me?"

"I love you will all my heart and soul. It has never changed for me. I will never love another."

"Then why are you trying to end this?"

"I will not hold you to me when your heart is not fully mine."

"But you have my heart, Thorn. You have had it for years. It is fully yours for eternity."

"What about your love for Zane?"

Ivy smiled up at Thorn. "My love for Zane is in friendship only. He has been a wonderful friend these last few years, but all I feel for him is the love of a dear friend."

"Ivy, I don't think you understand your true feelings. Also, you don't understand that Zane loves you too."

Ivy slid her hand over Thorn's cheek. She ran her thumb back and forth across his cheekbone. She stood on her tiptoes and gently kissed his lips.

"Thorn, my love, do not tell me my own feelings. I know who I love, and that is you, dearest. Zane and I only love each other as friends. We have been there for each other as friends. Nothing more. He tried to make you jealous. He understands how I love you and has tried to help me capture you. The picture he drew was of me talking about you. He told me stories of your time at school, and I expressed to him how much I missed you. Yes, it was a picture of a woman in love—a woman in love with you."

Thorn gathered Ivy into his arms and held her for a few moments. The tension eased from his body, soon replaced by relief. He was such an idiot. He almost lost her because of his own stupidity and jealousy. Marcus bent over to press a kiss to her forehead. Ivy tilted her head to look into his eyes. He finally saw for himself the love reflected there. He would no longer deny their love nor deny his affections toward her. She was his and nobody else's.

"I love you, my sweet Ivy."

"I love you, Marcus, with my whole heart."

"Can you ever forgive me?"

"There is nothing to ever forgive within our love."

Marcus lowered his head and took Ivy's mouth in a soul-searching kiss. His kiss became all-consuming as his love for her reached higher. He slid the blanket off her body as he lowered her to the cave floor. He needed to be inside her right this instant. He wanted the connection only she could give him.

Marcus reached down to spread her thighs open for him. He slowly slid inside her as far as he could go. He swallowed her moan as he kissed her deeper. As he made love to Ivy, he watched her eyes darken with passion with her love for him. His lips never left hers as he slid in and out of her, moving deeper inside her with every stroke. Their passion built higher with every stroke of their tongues, their bodies entwining with each other. He watched Ivy as she exploded with her love for him. The passion, desire, and love she held for him was there for him to see. He then went over the edge with his love for her.

Chapter Twenty-Two

WHEN IVY AWOKE AGAIN, it was to the touch of Marcus's tongue tracing the scar along the back of her thigh. His mouth nipped at it, and Ivy moaned. Marcus smiled at Ivy. He looked so sexy with his hair messed, staring at her with a look of love.

"Good evening, sleepyhead." He continued to trace the scar with his finger and mouth.

Ivy moaned at his touch. She craved this intimacy for years and now finally received it. She lay back as she let Marcus pleasure her. Ivy wanted to make love all day and night with Marcus. She could never getting enough of his affection.

"Do you remember the day you got this?" Marcus asked.

Ivy, unable to speak because of the wonderful things Marcus did with his tongue, nodded her head at him.

Marcus chuckled.

"You scared the life out of me that afternoon. When you came tumbling down the hill and caught on the branch, my heart stopped and started all over again. That was the day I realized how much you meant to me. I was no longer able to deny my love for you."

"But you yelled at me."

"I was furious when you followed us again. It was my fear that made me yell. You scared me as I watched you tumble and all the blood you lost. I suffered the same fear all over again on my ship. When I saw your scar on the ship, all my memories rushed back."

"Even though you yelled, you were still my hero. The way you wrapped my leg and carried me back to the house. Your soft voice whispered your assurances as you held me. It was the sound of your voice that brought me back on the ship. I heard your love for me in your voice both times, Marcus."

Marcus slid up her body and kissed her softly. He swept her hair away from her face and smiled at her.

"I will no longer deny my love for you ever again. I hope you won't ever grow tired of me telling you."

Ivy smiled at him. "Never."

"Can I confess something to you, Marcus?"

"You can confess anything, my dear."

"I found something by accident that confirmed your love for me while I was on the ship."

Marcus looked at her in confusion. He didn't know what she might have found to draw her to the conclusion of his love.

"What was that?"

"A poem."

Marcus smiled to himself. He realized what she referred to. He wrote it after the first kiss they shared. She must have snooped through his belongings to have found the poem. It was hidden deep in his chest. He only brought it out when missing her was too unbearable for him.

"I found it by accident. I wasn't snooping through your things, I swear. My hand bumped against the book as I tried to find something to wear. Please, forgive me."

"It is all right, my love. Anything of mine is yours. If I am not mistaken, I think the book belongs to you. It is I who should beg for your forgiveness."

"I thought I lost the book. I looked everywhere for it."

"After the kiss we shared in the garden, I came inside to leave for London. I noticed the book lying open in your room when I entered. I realized I shouldn't have gone in your bedroom, but I wanted to take a ribbon of yours as a keepsake. The book I gave you for your birthday that you always carried and read laid open on your nightstand. I wanted something you cherished to take with me. So, I slipped it inside my coat and left. Throughout the years I drew comfort from reading the poems you once read yourself."

"Enough comfort to write your own poem?"

It was Marcus's turn to blush. "Yes."

"It was beautiful. When I read the poem, I realized you loved me all those years ago. I don't understand why you left and why you have fought our love since we have left your ship."

"I left you all those years ago because I needed to grow up. It wasn't fair to leave you alone and waiting in fear for me to return from war. My father ordered me to leave you alone. Everybody wanted you to have a season in London. They thought you were too young to settle, and I was too wild. They were partly right. I don't think our love would have been strong enough then. It was too fresh."

"That explains then, but how do you explain your distance since our return to Thornhill Manor?"

"I felt guilty for taking advantage of you on my ship. I rushed you into an intimate relationship while you were recovering from your ordeal. On the carriage ride to Thornhill Manor, I promised myself I would give you time to heal. Since then I have been searching for Charles, or somebody has always been near, and I don't want to cause any rumors to tarnish your reputation."

"You are my fiancé, Marcus."

"I know, my dear, and that even makes me feel even guiltier."

"I don't understand."

"Of all the years I was away, I pictured coming back to court you. I wanted to win your love. I wanted to spoil you with picnics, take you for rides in the park, and waltz with you across the ballroom floors. You deserved a courtship, and I have given you none. I am forcing you into a quick wedding to protect you."

"Oh, you silly man. I do not need any of those things. I only need your love and your arms holding me close to you. You can spend the rest of our lives together courting me to your heart's desire."

"I don't deserve you."

"I know," Ivy kissed him softly across the lips, "but you have me, and I'm not going anywhere."

"Minx," Marcus laughed, deepening the kiss.

"You have finally returned to me with your love."

"And now our love will grow between the ivy and the thorns." Marcus quoted the last verse of his poem.

Marcus gathered Ivy deeper into his arms and held her, content with her by his side. They watched as it rained outside the cave. They would not be able to leave for a few hours until the storm stopped. Marcus ran his hands through her hair, spreading it out between his fingers. They lay there touching each other softly. They spoke no words to each other as they lay in peace with their love for each other.

Marcus needed to tell her what he discovered when he reached the cave. But he didn't want to lose the contentment he felt with her lying in his arms. It could wait. There was nothing they could do now since the rain fell harder. It would be hard to tell her. He was glad she had not wandered deeper into the cave, for the sight would have frightened her. He was scared himself of what it would mean if he hadn't seen the clue left for him. Only he realized what the clue meant. It held promise, but all the blood present could only mean one thing. He hoped he wasn't too late in his search for Charles.

When Ivy awoke, she was alone and wrapped in the blanket. Her sleepy eyes wandered the cave, looking for Thorn. She found him standing at the entrance to the cave as he stared into the dark night. The moonlight cast down upon him, and he looked deep in his thoughts. Ivy could tell something troubled him. She rose and slipped on his cotton shirt; it dropped past her knees. Ivy rolled the sleeves up her arms as she made her way over to him. When she reached his side, she slid her hands around to his front as she rested her head against his back. She held him, waiting for him to talk. She knew he would tell her what was on his mind, and she waited for him to find the words. He came here to look for Charles. Since he had not told her anything yet, she realized it was not good. As long as Marcus stayed by her side, she could deal with whatever he had to say. She understood it was just as hard for him because Charles was like a brother to him.

Marcus felt Ivy's arms wrap around him. He knew the moment she had awakened, as he was attuned to her every movement. It was time to tell her what he discovered. He reached around and brought her into the cradle of his arms. He held her in silence as he continued to watch the night sky.

The clouds moved swiftly, blocking the stars from shining down. He placed a kiss on Ivy's forehead. When her gaze rose, he saw the sadness in her eyes. She understood the news he must tell her wasn't promising, but she put on a brave front for him. He wanted to protect her from the danger in their life, but he understood they were stronger together than apart.

"What did you find, Marcus?" Ivy asked.

"Charles had been here since you saw him last. I think he came here to seek refuge from the beating."

"Where is he now? Why did he leave?"

"I don't know where he is, my dear. But he wasn't alone when he left."

"How do you know he wasn't alone?

"I found clues near the back of the cave. There were two sets of footprints, the second set were from someone with much smaller feet, perhaps a woman."

"How would a lady have knowledge of his hiding place? I didn't even know the location of this place until your father told me about it."

"From what I could tell, it appears somebody followed Charles to this location. Whoever she is, she has taken your brother to where we can't find him. But I don't think she means him harm. From what I could tell, it looks like she is taking care of his wounds."

"How did you learn this information?"

"Charles left me clues. After I secure you safely at Thornhill, I will continue my search for him with these new leads."

"I am coming with you. I am tired of not helping. I feel so useless."

"No, you are to remain at Thornhill Manor. I need you to be safe, and I can't keep you safe in my search for Charles. There are places I must search that are not safe for a lady. I won't risk your life. Promise me you will stay put, and I promise to bring Charles home safe to you. I realize I keep asking this, but I don't want anything to happen to you. You are my life. Plus, Shears and his men are still a threat to us."

"But I want to help, Marcus. What can I do to help?"

"You can read through his papers. Maybe you can learn more of his code. I have only cracked a some of it."

"Yes, I can do that. I will send a message to Zane in town to see if he will come to Thornhill and help me sort through Charles's papers."

Marcus gripped Ivy's arms and pushed her back from his body, so he could look more closely at her.

"You are to stay away from Maxwell, Ivy."

Ivy laughed nervously at Marcus's jealousy, but his tone suggested something darker than jealousy toward Zane.

"I thought we already discussed my relationship with Zane."

"I do not want you alone with him. Zane is involved with Captain Shears in some way. You are not safe in his company."

"You are being foolish. Zane is our friend. He would do nothing to harm any of us."

"You are being the foolish one, Ivy. I searched his room the other day. I found evidence of his involvement with Shears and the treason plot. He is not to be trusted."

"I don't believe you. He would never betray our country. You don't understand him like I do. I am going to send for him."

Marcus did not want to lose the precious ground they had mended. Their love was in a fragile stage right now. He wanted to show Ivy her thoughts were important to him. To agree, he would have to meet her halfway.

"I will agree to Zane's company at Thornhill to help with your investigation into Charles's papers on the condition you will never be left alone with him. A footman will be present at all times, and you will not go anywhere without a guard."

Ivy smiled at Marcus and squeezed his hands. "I will compromise with you on this. But you are wrong about Zane, and I will prove it to you."

Marcus clasped Ivy back into his arms. "I hope I am, for all of our sakes."

Chapter Twenty-Three

MARCUS AND IVY RODE back to Thornhill at a slow pace the next morning. Neither one of them wanted to lose the precious time they had left together. They were quiet, each lost in their own deep thoughts about the drama unfolding in their lives. But each time their eyes met, they recognized their thoughts were of the same. They took great comfort from that.

"Marcus, how come I never found this cave? I followed you boys everywhere when we were kids." Ivy asked.

"Charles and I discovered it by accident one afternoon while we were exploring. I think you were stuck in the house with Mother because of the rain." Marcus laughed at the memory.

"But all the times I followed you, I have never seen it before."

"Charles and I made a pact this would be our secret hiding place. We only ever snuck there when you weren't around. When we were younger, the cave was a place to escape when we needed to be alone."

Ivy didn't know whether to be hurt by this information or to understand even as boys they didn't always enjoy a little girl trailing after them, no matter how much she hero worshipped them. She pouted and flipped her head off to the side.

"Well, I didn't realize I was a nuisance to you two."

Marcus laughed at her pouting. "You knew darn well you were, and you enjoyed every minute."

Ivy's laugh rang out in the quiet air. "I sure did."

Ivy leaned over and kicked her heels lightly on the sides of her horse. The horse took off at a quick gallop with Ivy's laughter following in the winds. Thorn shook his head and smiled at her playfulness. He patted his horse. "I guess she wants to race, old boy. Should we give her one? Let's not beat her too badly though."

Pirate needed no other encouragement. He raced after Ivy in a dead sprint. Thorn kept Pirate reined in close to let Ivy win. They galloped into the yard and trotted to the stables. Thorn jumped from his horse to help Ivy down from hers before the stable boy arrived.

"Like I was saying, nothing but pure trouble," Thorn teased as he pulled Ivy into his arms.

Ivy laughed as she wrapped her arms around his shoulders. Thorn slid her body along the length of his and groaned lightly. Just holding Ivy in his arms made him want her. But they were back to needing to conduct themselves in accordance with the rules of society. Thorn would wait until later to continue this in private. He would not live without her any longer, but they must be very discreet. When he glanced around, he noticed no one was near and took her mouth in a deep kiss. Ivy moaned, leaned her body into his, and returned his kiss with promises of more.

"You will be trouble for the rest of our lives together, won't you, my dear?"

"You wouldn't have it any other way," Ivy replied, leaning in for another kiss.

Thorn grabbed her hand as they strolled into the house. They laughed and stole kisses on their way to the staircase. As they passed the library, they didn't notice Katherine standing inside the doorway with her arms crossed in disappointment. When they heard her clearing her throat for attention, they pulled apart quickly. They glanced at Katherine and then back at each other. They tried to keep straight faces but ended up breaking out in silly grins at being caught by his mother.

Thorn went over to his mother and gave her a peck on the cheek. "Good morning, Mother. How are you this fine day?"

Katherine turned and walked into the room, expecting them to follow.

"Please close the door, Marcus Edward Thornhill."

Thorn followed Ivy into the library, closing the door behind them after they entered. He looked over at his father lounging in the chair before the fireplace. His father shook his head at him and mouthed the word sorry. He realized he was in trouble when she spoke his full name. No child was ever safe when their parent spoke their middle name.

Katherine waved her arm for them to sit on the couch. Thorn grabbed Ivy's hand and intertwined his fingers with hers as they waited for Katherine's lecture. He couldn't wipe the smile from his face even if he tried. He knew what his mother would say, but he didn't care. Thorn finally felt content and secure of Ivy's love for him and of his love for her.

"Do you two children have any idea of what kind of scandal you might have caused being alone together? I have done everything in my power to keep hush of the scandal of Ivy's disappearance with this betrothal ball and wedding. Now, our guests have arrived for the ball the evening you two go missing, and then you reappear together kissing near the stables. How will you explain your actions?"

Thorn brought their hands up to his mouth and placed a kiss on Ivy's fingers. He then rose and embraced his mother. "We love each other,

Mother. That is all there is to say." He then walked over to his father, bowed, and shook his hand. "Thank you, Father, for your wonderful gift."

"How is your father involved with your disappearance?"

"He sent Ivy after me. We have worked out the confusion we were having in our relationship. We now understand how strong our love is for each other."

"Well of course you two love each other. You have for ages since you both were young. What did you need to figure out that would put your reputations at risk?" Katherine asked Ivy and Thorn, looking back and forth between them. She turned on Hamilton and fired off questions for him. "Why would you send Ivy out alone with the danger she is in? Why would you risk more scandal on them?"

Hamilton rose from his chair pulled Katherine into his arms.

"My dear, Ivy was never alone. I sent Peter with her until she met with Thorn. These young kids needed a little nudge to settle their misunderstandings before they walked down the aisle in doubt. As you can see, they have finally done that. You need not worry, my dear. No one knows they were alone, and nobody saw them return. You handled their excuses brilliantly last evening. They have now returned, and nobody is the wiser."

Ivy rushed over to Katherine and held her hands. "Please, forgive me, Katherine. I never meant any trouble for you. You have been nothing but kind and generous toward me. I don't want to lose your love as a mother. I promise I won't cause you any more trouble before the wedding."

Katherine squeezed Ivy's hands. "You will never lose my love, child. I can see the love pouring from both of you. I understand you both struggled with this love for each other over the last few years and have not known how to handle it. You bring me joy that you both woken to the precious gift set before you."

Ivy kissed Hamilton on the cheek. "Thank you, Father."

Hamilton laughed and winked at Katherine. "It was my pleasure, miss." Ivy watched as Katherine blushed a deep shade of red under Hamilton's perusal.

Everybody laughed at Hamilton's teasing.

"Now everybody please get upstairs and change your clothes. There are guests to entertain and last-minute touches for the ball to take care of," Katherine ordered them. Hamilton winked at Ivy and Thorn as he followed Katherine out of the library.

Thorn pulled Ivy into his arms and kissed her gently. He smiled at her with all the happiness inside him.

"I love you."

"I love you too, Thorn."

"I guess we had better follow Mother's rules for a few more days. Then we can defy them all we want," Thorn said with a wink.

Ivy laughed. "Do you promise?"

"Oh, I most definitely promise. You better leave first. I will follow shortly," Thorn said.

Ivy began to walk out of the library and then turned to find Thorn watching her with a silly grin on his face. She smiled sadly at him. "We will find him, won't we?"

Thorn's smile slipped, and he nodded his head at Ivy in the affirmative.

Ivy nodded her head at Thorn and left the library, pulling the door shut behind her.

Chapter Twenty-Four

THORN SLID INTO THE chair Hamilton occupied a few minutes ago. The happiness he felt soon deflated at Ivy's departure. He ran his hand down his face, pinching his thumb and fingers into his eyes. He kept his eyes closed as he thought of the next step in finding Charles. When he slid his hand into his pocket, he pulled out a ladies' handkerchief. It had been white at one time, but it was now covered in dried blood. He suspected the blood to be Charles's. It wasn't the bloody handkerchief that had Thorn puzzled but the initials and embroidery adorned on it. He had seen this before but needed it cleaned to confirm his suspicions. If it belonged to whom he thought it did, then there were more facets to this treason than he could even imagine. He hoped that whatever humanity remained with the owner of this handkerchief they would apply to the care of Charles. If not, then there was nothing he could do to save him.

Thorn walked along the hallway and ran into Cleaves.

"Please, have this washed and returned to me. I need you to do this yourself. Do not let anybody else see this, especially Lady Ivy. Also, send for Sammy right way."

"Yes, my lord. Sammy arrived during the night and has been waiting for you. I will send him to your rooms immediately."

Thorn walked to his rooms. He hoped Sammy had some news for him on Shears's whereabouts. Thorn didn't have to wait long before Sammy knocked on his door. After he dismissed his valet, Thorn sat behind his desk. Sammy pulled up a chair and sat down. He stretched his legs out in front of him rubbing his sore leg.

"I'm sorry you need to keep traveling here, Sammy. I think we are getting close to finding Charles. Is your leg troubling you today?"

"It is just the weather, Captain. The rain tends to make it ache a bit more than usual. I have been waiting for you since last night. Did you run into trouble?"

Thorn smiled to himself. "You could say that Sammy. But nothing to trouble yourself over, as it was definitely the good kind of trouble."

Sammy shook his head in confusion but didn't ask any further. The captain seemed to have enjoyed his trouble, whatever it was.

"Were you able to track our good friend Shears?"

"Even better than that, Captain. I saw with my own two eyes him and that friend of yours, Maxwell meeting by the docks. I followed them down an alley and into an abandoned warehouse. They did not see me, but I saw them."

"Did you hear anything that was said?"

"They were talking about the delivery of a shipment. Shears threatened Maxwell to come through for him with details of Mallory's hideout. I think Maxwell might know where Mallory is hidden."

"Was there anything in the warehouse?"

"Yes, it is full of weapons. There are enough weapons there to start a war here on English soil, Captain."

"Can you find this warehouse again?"

"Yes, but we will need a lot of men to overtake it. Shears's men heavily guard the warehouse."

"I want you to post a few men to watch it and inform me if there is any sudden activity."

"Yes, Capt'n. What are you going to do about Maxwell?"

"Did you see where he went after his meeting with Shears?"

"Yes, I followed him out of town to a small cottage set back in the woods. When he knocked on the door, a young lady opened the door and rushed him inside. He looked behind him after he entered, like he tried to see if he had been followed."

"Do you think he saw you?"

"No, Captain. He only stayed for an hour. He returned to the inn and has been there ever since. I've got men guarding both exits, and I have talked to the chambermaids. He has taken all his meals in his room."

"Did you recognize the lady at the cottage?"

"I did not get a good look at her. Do you know who she is?"

"I have a good idea. I will know more soon."

There was a knock on the door, and Thorn bade them to enter. It was Cleaves who brought him the clean handkerchief. After the butler left the room, Thorn opened the material and saw what he feared when he first found it. It bore the initials RL.

"Does this look familiar to you, Sammy?" Thorn held the cloth for Sammy to inspect.

Sammy touched the soft linen, turning it over in his hands. He rubbed his fingers across the embroidered letters. When recognition replaced curiosity, he looked to meet Thorn's eyes. Thorn nodded his head at Sammy's unspoken question. They both realized what this meant. She had sworn revenge on them, and it seemed she placed it into action in the form of Charles.

"Where did you find this?"

"It was at a place that only Charles and I hold knowledge of. She was there with him and now she has him. I need you to take me to her, Sammy."

"Lady Ivy will be excited to learn we have found Lord Mallory."

"I do not want her to know any of this until we have him back here safely."

"Yes, Capt'n."

"Can you ride?"

"Yes. Anything for Lady Ivy. It is time to bring her brother home."

Thorn rose from his desk and pulled open a drawer. He dragged out two pistols and loaded them, handing one over to Sammy. He grabbed the other pistol, and they left his room. They escaped to the stables without running into Ivy or his parents. After they saddled their horses, Sammy led Thorn to the cottage. He hoped they weren't too late.

~~~~~

Ivy snuck along the hallway toward Thorn's room, on guard for any sign of Katherine. She'd managed to avoid her so far. She wanted to greet their guests with Thorn. When her maid told her Thorn wasn't downstairs yet, Ivy figured he was still in his room getting ready. She knocked lightly on his door to announce herself, then slipped inside quickly.

"Thorn, are you in here?" Ivy whispered.

When there was no reply, Ivy ventured farther into the room. She noticed his desk had been disturbed, like he had left in a hurry. There was a white piece of linen lying on top of his papers. Ivy lifted it and realized it was a woman's handkerchief. It was embroidered with roses around the edges and had the owner's initials sewn in. RL. Who was RL, and what did she mean to Thorn? Was it an old lover's memento? Why would he have this lying around after all they had confessed and shared with each other? Old doubts crept into Ivy's head. Would she ever feel secure in their love?

Ivy heard voices outside the room. The servants searched for her. It would not look good to be found in Thorn's room. She grabbed the handkerchief, sliding it into the pocket of her dress. She slid inside his closet to hide. The door to Thorn's room opened and closed. When Ivy peeked her head to check if the coast was clear, Zane slipped inside the room and walked over to Thorn's desk. Ivy's fingers slipped on the door, and it slowly opened, revealing her hiding space.   Zane listened as the door to the closet creaked open slowly. He noticed Ivy tucked among Thorn's overcoats. She'd almost caught him searching through Thorn's desk. He didn't know how he would have explained himself out of the mess. While it frustrated him that he couldn't look for what Thorn had stolen from his room at the inn and for information on the treason plot, he was relieved nobody caught him. He could explain himself to Ivy and she would believe him. But he realized once she told Thorn, Thorn wouldn't believe him. He was already on thin ice with Thorn and didn't need him to be any more suspicious than he already was.

Zane heard the rattling of Thorn's bedroom door and realized that unless he acted quickly, someone would discover them where they shouldn't be. Also, being caught together would cause Ivy a whole new set of problems she didn't need. He slipped into the closet with her and covered her mouth with his hand.

"Don't make a sound. Somebody else is coming into the room," Zane whispered into Ivy's ear as he held her close.

Ivy nodded her head to let Zane know she understood. Zane sighed as his body relaxed into hers. He lowered his hand from her mouth but kept her close to his body.

They stood there listening as somebody searched through Thorn's desk. They heard the doors slide open and the rustling of papers. Then just as soon as the person entered the room, they left again. Either the person found what they looked for or did not want to be found in the room. With servants and guests wandering all over the house, they understood they would not have much time to search. Zane and Ivy were unable to tell who was in the room without being caught themselves. Zane knew what the person searched for without knowing who the person was. Thorn held a vital piece of information about the treason plot in his possession. Zane only hoped whoever was in the room did not find it, and if they did find it, he hoped they would not try to use it.

Zane stroked his hand along Ivy's hair and pulled her closer. Ivy stared at him in confusion. He had never been this intimate with her before. When he lowered his head and took her mouth in a soft gentle kiss, Ivy was never more surprised. He kissed her long and slow, testing the waters. When Ivy didn't respond to the kiss, Zane deepened the kiss in desperation. The kiss tasted nice to Ivy, but it didn't hold the passion she felt for Thorn. Zane pulled away and ran his thumb across Ivy's lips.

"Nothing?" he questioned.

Ivy shook her head in response.

"Why?" she asked.

"A man has to try, doesn't he?"

"Why?" she asked again.

"Why? That is a very loaded question, my dear."

"Can you answer it?"

"I wanted to satisfy my curiosity, to see if you care for me as I care for you."

Ivy reached her hand to cup his cheek.

"You don't care for me in that sense either. So why did you kiss me?"

"I have always been attracted to you, Ivy. I knew you were off limits and wanted to at least give it a try. If not, I would always regret that I didn't."

"Except you also felt nothing."

"Believe me, my dear, I felt more than nothing. I would have to be dead not to feel anything with you in my arms and my lips on yours. But no, my dear friend, I felt no passion between us. Are we still friends?"

Ivy laughed and stood to kiss him on the cheek. "The very best of them."

Zane grabbed Ivy's hand and led her from the closet.

"Who was in here and what were they searching for?" Ivy asked Zane.

"I don't know, but they did not stay long. Our mysterious guest either found what they wanted or they didn't want to get caught."

"What are you doing in Thorn's room?"

"I was going to ask you the same, my dear."

Ivy stared at the piece of fabric in her hand and sadness entered her eyes. A tear slid along her cheek, and she wiped it away.

"I came to find Thorn, but I found this on his desk instead."

Zane reached to grab the linen from Ivy's hand. He noticed the initials on it and realized where Thorn was. This was a disaster. Things were out of his control, and he needed a plan to gain them back. But first he had to ease Ivy's mind and lay her fears to rest.

"Who do you think she is? Does he love her?"

"He loves you, my dear. There is nobody else, nor has there ever been anybody else."

"Who is she to him?"

Zane slid the handkerchief into his pocket and pulled Ivy's into his arms. He gave her a friendly hug. He must remove Ivy from Thorn's room without being seen. Then he needed to return to the woman who the handkerchief belonged to. He hoped he wasn't too late.

"I will find out for you. Meanwhile, we need to leave this room without anybody seeing either one of us."

Zane strode to the door and opened it a crack. When he noticed there was nobody in the hallway, he motioned for Ivy to leave. Ivy slipped out of the room and rushed along the hallway to put distance between them. Zane glanced over his shoulder at the desk in regret. He realized he had to leave or else get caught. He hoped whoever was in the room did not find what they searched for.

~~~~~

As Thorn and Sammy approached the road leading to the cottage, they slid off their horses and tied them to a tree. They decided to sneak up to the cottage on foot. When they arrived at the cottage, they noticed there didn't seem to be any movement inside. Thorn motioned for Sammy to head around back, and he would enter through the front. Thorn slid the door open as quietly as he could. He winced when the door let out a loud squeak. He raised his gun, ready to defend himself, but nobody rushed out at him. Thorn kept close to the walls as he searched the cottage, only to find it empty. Thorn went to the back bedroom, hoping to find Charles when he opened the door. Instead, he found an empty bed and bandages strewn across the floor. There was no sign of anybody.

"The place is empty, Captain. Not a soul in sight," Sammy said from the open doorway.

"It appears they left in a hurry. The question is to where?"

Thorn searched the room for any clue if Charles or his mystery lady had been there. Whoever was here made sure they left no evidence behind. They came to another dead end.

"Help me search the house and grounds for any clues we can find. Then we will need to hurry back to Thornhill. I have a ball I must attend tonight. I need you to stand guard tonight and look for any suspicious activity. You must be on the lookout for the girl and have the men watch Maxwell like a hawk. He is knee-deep involved in this, and I don't think for the good."

"Where do you think they disappeared to?"

"I'm not sure, Sammy. I sense she will show herself t at the ball tonight, and I want us to be ready for her."

Thorn and Sammy searched the house and grounds but came up empty-handed. As they traveled back to Thornhill, they tried to piece together the puzzle and place the pieces where they thought they might fit. At this moment, Thorn realized he could only trust a few people. Until they located Charles, nobody was safe from Shears's plan.

Chapter Twenty-Five

THORN WAITED IMPATIENTLY FOR Ivy to arrive downstairs. He paced back and forth at the bottom of the staircase, nervous as a schoolboy. This would be his one chance to gift Ivy all the things he wanted to do with her as if he courted her. He sent a dozen red roses to her room earlier as she prepared for the ball. She replied with a simple thank you note written on her stationary, sprayed with her perfume. He kept the note in his pocket now.

He gave the orchestra instructions for the first dance to be a waltz. Thorn could not wait to hold her in his arms as he whisked her across the ballroom floor. Thorn tugged his timepiece out of his pocket and noted the late hour. They would have to arrive in line soon to receive their guests. He wanted a few moments alone with Ivy before the ball began.

Thorn heard a noise at the top of the staircase and noticed Ivy waiting, ready to descend. She held onto the banister and clutched her fan in her other hand, looking as nervous as he felt. Thorn stared at her, dumbfounded. She was a vision to behold. Her long blonde hair was secured in curls, softly framing her face as they cascaded along her back. The soft blue material of her dress shaped her body into that of a goddess. It flowed around her curves in soft waves. Her dress was all the different shades of blue blended together. All the blues matched the ocean and open sky he sailed on for the last seven years. His Ivy dressed to make his heart sail to her open sea. He realized he should help her down the stairs, but he stood there like a young lad staring at his first pretty lady. Ivy floated down the stairs to him with a sweet innocent smile mixed with a bit of minx.

Ivy smiled to herself as she made her way down the stairs to Thorn. She was nervous when she left her room, but when she came to the top of the staircase and saw Thorn pacing back and forth, she realized she wasn't the only one nervous. He was dressed in dark evening attire—black trousers that hugged his thighs, dark black evening coat, and a blue waistcoat underneath that matched her dress perfectly. He wore a white cravat with a blue sapphire pin in the middle. His hair was pulled back in a queue. He looked so different from the captain of his ship. Now he was a marquess of the ton on his way to a ball. His ball no less. As she continued watching him, she realized she would take him any way she could have him. Because he was Thorn. Then when he stared at her full of desire and love, Ivy knew in her heart there was nothing to be nervous about. By the way Thorn gazed at her, she realized this would be an evening they would never forget. Ivy stopped near the bottom of the stairs, so she was level with Thorn. She leaned forward and placed a soft kiss on his lips.

"Thank you for the beautiful roses Marcus."

"Your welcome, my dear. I hoped you enjoyed them while you dressed for the ball."

"I did."

"There are no words to describe the beautiful vision you are tonight, my love."

Ivy blushed as she smoothed her hand over her dress.

"Do you like the colors, Marcus?"

"Yes, my dear. Your choice makes my heart full."

Marcus lowered himself to one knee and reached for Ivy's hand. He slid his hand into his pocket and pulled out a sapphire ring surrounded by diamonds. As he slid the ring onto Ivy's finger, he placed a kiss on her hand. He rose and gathered Ivy into his arms.

"Now you are mine," he said as he lowered his head and took Ivy's lips in a passionate kiss. The kiss told Ivy of his love for her and how much tonight meant to him. It also held a promise of more to come. He felt Ivy clutch to him and return his kiss with the same amount of passion, desire, and love.

"Are you ready to greet our guests, my love?" Marcus asked.

Ivy nodded. She wanted to confront Marcus on the handkerchief, but it was not the appropriate moment. She didn't want any reason to ruin this evening. Tonight would be all the nights she wished with Marcus rolled into one. It could wait until tomorrow. He loved her, and she understood that. Whoever the other lady was, she was part of his past. Ivy was his future.

Marcus and Ivy strolled to the front of the house to join his parents and Ivy's father to receive their guests. The guests already filed into the house. His mother had outdone herself. Also, this ball would settle all the gossip to rest, and nobody would miss a chance to see how the engaged couple behaved with each other. He sure hated to disappoint the ton, but disappointed they would be. All they would witness tonight were two souls very much in love with one another.

After they greeted their guests, Ivy's friends dragged her off to the side for some friendly gossip, while Thorn's friends welcomed him home. Thorn listened in boredom as he watched Ivy talk to her friends. The ladies admired the ring he gave her. Once her friends moved on, the gentlemen swarmed to her side.

Thorn joined Ivy, staking his claim. He should have known all the eligible bachelors would flock to her. Her dance card would be full tonight, but before that happened, he had a surprise for her.

"Excuse me, gentlemen, but I need to steal my bride-to-be away from your adoring attention."

All the men groaned as Ivy blushed his new favorite color—red. He would never grow tired of the color and would make sure she turned that shade every day for the rest of their lives.

"Bugger off, Thornhill. You get her for the rest of your days, let us enjoy her last night of freedom," Maxwell commented.

Thorn slid Ivy's hand into the crook of his arm as he took her away from all her admirers. He chose to ignore Maxwell's comment.

"Slow down, Thorn, where are you taking me?"

"You shall see in a moment, my dear."

He stopped in the middle of the dance floor and gathered Ivy into his arms. He gazed as the confusion in her eyes gave away to understanding. Her smile lifted with love.

"May I have this waltz?" Marcus asked.

Ivy nodded her head, her emotions choking her ability to talk. Marcus's thoughtfulness brought tears of joy to her eyes. He was courting her tonight.

Marcus nodded to the orchestra to begin the waltz. The music started, and Marcus danced Ivy across the floor. Their bodies became one as they danced to the powerful melody. Ivy melted into his arms as he led her through the steps. She felt like she floated through the air in his arms. Ivy understood how much this dance meant to Marcus. It was all the dances they'd missed together through the years. It was also the dance they would remember in the years to come.

The ton stood off to the side of the dance floor as they admired the love expressed in their dance. Some watched in envy, others watched in awe. There were those who wished that kind of love swept them away. Then there were the others whose jealousy wrapped them in their own misery, and they couldn't appreciate the beauty of the dancers.

When the dance ended, Marcus pulled Ivy to him and kissed her deeply for the whole ton to see. Ivy returned his kiss then backed away, laughing as the crowd broke out in applause and laughter. Katherine quickly ordered the orchestra into another reel and shook her head at Marcus in disapproval but winked her real approval. Young men rushed to Ivy's side to claim her for the next dance, and Marcus knew his time with her was done for now. He gave Ivy over to her admirers with a promise in her ear. He whispered he would steal her away later for a kiss or two.

Thorn sauntered over to the bar, set in the ballroom's corner. He ordered a whiskey and watched as a young pup led Ivy onto the dance floor. He smiled as she danced a country reel, her cheeks flushed with excitement. As he admired his bride dancing, he noticed Maxwell headed toward him.

"We need to talk, Thornhill."

"Whatever you have to say can wait. I will not ruin Ivy's evening by fighting with you."

"You have already ruined Ivy's night, only she isn't showing it."

Thorn looked at Maxwell in confusion and saw the anger on his face. He then transferred his gaze over to Ivy, who watched them as her partner twirled her around. He caught the hurt in her eyes and noticed her shaking her head at Maxwell. Thorn glanced back and forth between the two and then nodded his head at Maxwell to follow him. Thorn led the way to his father's study. As soon as he strolled through the door, he turned on Maxwell.

"What is this all about?"

"Perhaps, you can tell me," Maxwell said as he produced the linen handkerchief from his pocket.

Thorn stared down at the piece of cloth in Maxwell's hand. Had Ivy seen it?

"Do you want to inform me how that came to be in your possession?"

"Oh, I would love to. I snuck into your room to retrieve something that was mine. I think you know what I am referring to, and I will want it returned. Then I heard somebody else sneaking into your room. I only did what any person would do and hid in your closet. But low and behold I ran into company inside your closet. Now, who be it for me to complain on said company. It was heaven to be stuck in there with her in such tight quarters. Believe me, when I say I took complete advantage of the situation."

Thorn advanced at Maxwell in anger. He pulled him close by his cravat and snarled into his face.

"You better not be saying what I think you're saying."

"Calm down, old man. Nothing happened. But it was not for lack of trying on my part. But her heart belongs to you. I did not stand a chance." Maxwell yanked himself away from Thorn, straightened his cravat, and smoothed his dinner jacket back in place.

Thorn stalked over to his desk and unlocked the drawer. He removed the item Maxwell referred to and slid it across the desk.

Maxwell picked it up, ran his thumb across the smooth surface, and slid the object into his pocket. He nodded his head at Thorn in thanks for returning it.

"I will not explain it to you. Maybe one day, but not today. You had no right to steal this from by bag. There could have been dire circumstances if this fell into the wrong hands."

"Maybe you shouldn't be so careless with your treasures," Thorn taunted.

"I could say the same to you," Maxwell replied as he waved the handkerchief. He threw it on the desk.

"Did she see it?" Thorn asked as he lifted it and slid it into his pocket.

"She is the one who gave it to me. She was in tears and was afraid your heart lies with another lady from your past. Is she correct?"

"The lady is from my past but not in the sense Ivy imagines. I think she holds the key to Charles's whereabouts. But you are already aware of this information, aren't you? You know the location of the lady—and Charles. My only question to you is why?"

Before Thorn received his answers from Maxwell, his mother entered the room.

"There you are. We have searched all over for you. It is time for your father's toast. You boys can talk later."

Katherine ushered them out of the study and back into the ballroom. Thorn turned to Maxwell and said, "We will finish this discussion later." Maxwell nodded at him and disappeared into the crowd.

~~~~~~

Ivy caught glimpses of the young lady all evening. It seemed wherever she went, the lady followed her. It was not like she was hard to miss. A red creation graced her figure, which made the men drool and the women green with envy. The dress fit her like a glove, tight in all the right places. Ivy envied her too. The lady appeared comfortable and at ease in such a concoction. Ivy would feel self-conscious in something so daring.

But it wasn't the dress that kept drawing Ivy's attention to the lady. It was the choker she wore around her neck that drew her attention. It looked familiar, and she needed to get a closer look. If it was what Ivy thought it was, then the lady would have questions to answer. Ivy sent her dance partner away to get her a drink of punch. As soon as he left her, Ivy started toward the lady in the red dress.

As Ivy approached the lady, she knew. The choker was her mother's necklace. The bright red ruby with little diamonds surrounding the stone winked at Ivy as she stared at the familiar heirloom. There was only one reason why she would wear the piece of jewelry, and it was because of Charles. Charles never went anywhere without the necklace. He always wore it under his shirt. The lady must know where Charles was. He must have sent her here to help him. Ivy reached for the lady's hand and squeezed softly.

"Where is he?" she whispered.

"Where is who, madam?" the lady answered pulling her hands out of Ivy's grasp.

"Charles."

"I am sorry. I do not know of any Charles. You must have me mistaken for somebody else."

"No, I know you have knowledge of where he is. You are wearing his necklace."

The lady reached to run her fingers across the choker, looking guilty.

"You are mistaken madam. This is an old family heirloom."

"Yes, from my family. Did he send you here? Who are you? Why are you here?" Ivy questioned her in desperation.

The lady looked over Ivy's shoulder and turned pale. Ivy turned to glance at who she stared at. But the overcrowded room made it difficult to notice who scared the lady. When Ivy turned back, the lady disappeared. Ivy stood on her toes to search over the guests' heads. But she was unable to locate her. It was if she'd vanished in plain sight. Ivy needed to find Thorn and tell him about the mystery lady. He would help find her. If they found her, then she could lead them to Charles.

Ivy appeared at Thorn's side looking distressed.

"What is the matter, my dear?"

"Thorn, I found somebody who knows where Charles is."

"Who did you find?"

"I don't know who she is. She disappeared. I need your help to find her. She is wearing Mother's ruby necklace. The lady is wearing a red dress and has a French accent."

Thorn knew who Ivy described. How did she sneak into the ball was his main question. He posted Sammy and his men all over to watch for her. He wouldn't put it past Maxwell to be the culprit. Thorn didn't want Ivy to find her; it would only put her in more danger. Thorn didn't know how stable their uninvited guest was, and he needed to get Ivy safely out of the way.

"I will find her, Ivy. I need you to stay here."

"No, I want to help you. She has information on Charles."

Thorn needed to think of a way to keep Ivy out of harm's way. He saw his mother approaching them.

"Mother, why don't you take Ivy to freshen up before Father's speech?"

"That is a fabulous idea, Thorn," Katherine said as she ushered Ivy to a receiving room to freshen up.

Ivy glared at him over her shoulder as she walked away with his mother. He hoped his mother could keep Ivy distracted long enough for him to find the lady Ivy described. She was somewhere at the ball, and he would find her. As soon as he found her, she would lead him to Charles.

He decided to walk along the perimeter of the room. He sensed she would not want to draw notice to herself and would keep to the shadows. The question was why she risked coming to the ball. She had to realize somebody would question why she was here. From what Ivy said, she waved a red flag, so she wanted to draw attention to herself. Since she wore the Mallory ruby necklace, she wished to be seen. Did Charles send her here?

He spotted her by the balcony windows. She was the red flag tempting the bull for attention. Thorn slid behind her and caught her by surprise. He leaned to whisper in her ear.

"Would you like a breath of fresh air, my lady?"

Thorn waited as she turned in surprise. She started to back away from him, searching for an exit. He grabbed her arm before she could dart away and dragged her close to him.

"Going somewhere?" he asked.

"Let me go, Captain Thornhill. I am not your prisoner anymore."

"You were never my prisoner, Ms. LeClair. I only helped your father. I did not harm him."

"You killed him, and I am here to avenge him any way I can."

"Is Charles Mallory part of your revenge?"

She paled at the mention of Charles's name. A look of confusion flashed in her eyes. Thorn could not interpret the look. It seemed for a split second she showed true emotion at the mention of Charles's name. Then the glare of anger and revenge entered her eyes again. She pulled at her arm, trying to break free. He needed to get her out of here before she caused a scene—and before Ivy spotted them. He pushed opened the balcony doors and pulled her through.

"Let me go, Captain Thornhill," she hissed.

"Not until you answer my questions, Ms. LeClair," Thorn growled as he ushered her down the stairs and into the garden.

Thorn led Raina LeClair deep into the garden, away from the ball and the guests wandering the grounds. She struggled in his hold, but Thorn clenched her arm, only letting her go once they reached the back gate. It was dark this far back in the garden, with only the moon to guide them. He released her and watched while she searched for a way to escape. He leaned against the gate as he kept an eye on her movements. When she finally realized she had nowhere to run, she rushed at him in anger.

She started beating on his chest. But Thorn would not have any of it, so he grabbed her wrists and held them tightly in his grasp. He wrenched her close and glared into her face. She whimpered from his tight hold. When he saw fear mixed with anger in her eyes, Thorn loosened his hold.

"Are you ready to answer my questions, Ms. LeClair?"

She remained silent, glaring at him with her eyes half lowered. She turned her head to the side to ignore him as she moved her arms, trying to loosen his hold on her wrists. As she struggled, Thorn only tightened his grip more.

She sighed with defeat. "Yes, Captain."

"Are you working with Shears?"

She glared into his face, smiling with scorn. "Oui."

"Why? Your father would not have wanted you involved with him."

"Do not speak of my father. You killed him. Shears promised me my revenge on you."

"Raina, I was helping your father get out of France. England would have protected your father and you from men like Shears. We were double-crossed. I am sorry for that, but I did not kill your father."

"But in the end, we were not protected were we, Captain?"

"I can help you now, Raina. Take me to Charles and we can protect you from Shears."

"Nobody is safe from Shears. He has too many connections. Can you not see how protected he is? There are men in your own government who protect him and destroy people like me for fun."

"I have strong connections myself, as does Charles. I know you have been caring for him."

Her eyes clouded over at the mention of Charles's name. She became even more guarded and alert. Thorn scrutinized her emotions as they flashed across her face whenever he mentioned Charles. He decided he needed to talk about Charles more to break her.

"I know he needs care, Raina. When I was at the cave, I saw the blood. He must have lost a good amount. I also saw the bandages at your cottage. I know you have been trying to care for him yourself. Let me help him. If he doesn't get the help he needs soon, he could die. Will your revenge be complete then?"

Raina gasped at the image Thorn described. Tears slowly slid from her eyes. Her body stopped struggling against his hold. Finally, he got through to her.

"I will take you to him. We must hurry though. Shears is planning to gather the weapons from his warehouse tonight and put his plan into action."

"Where is Charles?"

"Down in a cave on the beach. Maxwell moved us there after Shears found our location at the cottage."

"Did he move Mallory where Shears could find him? How deep is Maxwell's involvement with Shears?" Thorn questioned Raina.

"His involvement runs deep, but not enough to risk his friend's life. The earl was helping me save Charles. Please hurry. I do not want his blood on my hands. I could not live with myself."

Thorn heard the raw emotion in Raina's voice when she spoke of Charles. She cared for him, it was obvious. But did she care enough for him to save him? Was she leading Thorn to Charles, or did she play out her revenge by leading him into Shears's hands? Either way, he must try to save Charles's life.

He loosened his hold on her wrists as he kept her close to his side. He still did not trust her enough to release her. After he sent out a sharp whistle, he waited for his men to join him. As they came out of their hiding places in the garden, he instructed them on his plan.

"Lead the way, Ms. LeClair. I hope we are not too late."

Chapter Twenty-Six

IVY GLARED AT THORN over her shoulder. As soon as she was free
from Katherine, she would find the mystery lady herself. She was tired of
being left behind. Charles was her brother, and he needed her. Why else
would he have sent her the message he did? Who was the lady afraid of?
Somebody spooked her.

Ivy let Katherine fuss over her. Katherine chattered about the
success of the ball as they freshened Ivy's hair and gown. As she talked, Ivy
thought of an idea how to get away from her.

"Katherine, can you please fetch me a new pair of slippers? I'm
afraid I have worn these things through with all the dancing."

"Of course, my dear. You rest while I send for Mabel to get you a
new pair."

As soon as Katherine left the room to call for Mabel, Ivy slipped out
and ran down the hall. She climbed the stairs to look out over the entire
ballroom. Ivy noticed the fabric of the dress before she saw the girl. The red
stood out against the white curtains she stood by. She observed the girl's
arm held by a gentleman, and they were arguing. Ivy stood on her tiptoes to
catch a glimpse of the man. She gasped as she realized it wasn't just any
man that held the girl's arm possessively but the hand of her fiancé. Ivy
realized they argued, and Thorn glanced around the room to make sure

nobody watched him as he slid them through the balcony doors. She clutched the railing for support as her knees went weak from her distress.

Ivy straightened herself and dashed down the stairs. She would not get answers by playing the damsel in distress. As she hurried after them, she slid through the balcony doors and watched them take the stairs to the gardens. She continued after them but lost them through the maze. Their dark clothes blended into the night.

Ivy wandered through the maze, hoping to spot them. With no luck finding them, she decided to return to the party. She would find Zane, and he would help her search for the mystery lady and Thorn. Then hopefully it would lead them to Charles.

Ivy heard footsteps behind her, but when she turned, she saw nothing but darkness. She'd wandered farther into the maze than she realized. There were no lights to guide her along the path. Ivy rushed her pace, but the footsteps drew closer. She felt frightened for the first time at Thornhill Manor. She lowered her hand, bunched her skirts, and ran. The footsteps ran after her. She could her them gaining on her. When she saw the lights, she realized she was close to the manor. Suddenly, somebody grabbed her from behind and brought her against a hard, male chest.

She smelled the scent of sandalwood on her abductor. He wrapped an arm around Ivy and held her close while his other hand covered her mouth. He pulled her back into the trees to hide them. Ivy fought against his restraints and tried to bite at the hand covering her mouth. She tasted the fear in her mouth. His hold on her tightened while he shushed her to be quiet. The voice sounded familiar, but she was unable to figure out who held her. His voice was muffled in her hair. He leaned his head to whisper in her ear.

"Stay still and don't make a single sound. Do you understand?"

Ivy nodded her head she understood. Her body sagged against her captor. She recognized the voice as Zane's and felt safe in his arms. He still held her tightly to his body. Ivy sensed how alert he was when his arms tensed around her. He seemed to be prepared for whatever trouble laid in wait for them. As soon as Ivy relaxed in Zane's hold, she heard voices whispering in the darkness.

"Where did she go?"

"I don't know, Captain, she was here a second ago. She was within my grasp."

"Well you've lost her. Comb the area and be quick about it. We don't want Captain Thornhill to catch us here."

As the men searched for her, Ivy recognized the voice of Captain Shears. She shivered at the sound of his voice. Ivy clutched her hands around Zane's arm in fear of being found. Zane backed them farther into the shadows. He understood her fear when his arms wrapped around her to keep her hidden and protected.

"She is nowhere to be found, Captain."

"We need to return to the ship. I have other things to attend to this evening. The lovely Lady Ivy will have to wait for my attention. She will have it soon enough." Captain Shears laughed.

Zane waited until the footsteps disappeared before he brought them out of the shadows. He withdrew his hand from her mouth. As he started to pull away from Ivy, she swayed in his arms. He gathered her in closer as his hand caressed her back in comfort. He closed his eyes as he locked this memory in his heart to last him forever.

She felt so right in his arms. He knew it was wrong to care for her this way; she was his friend's fiancée. Still, she was a lady he came to care for and admire over the years. He realized he clouded their friendship with his desire to be with her. As he savored these few stolen moments with her, he realized they would have to last him a lifetime. For after tonight, her feelings toward him would change, and in the end, he would probably lose the most important thing he valued the most. Her friendship.

"Are you all right, Ivy?"

"I will be fine as soon as I find Thorn. Thank you for saving me from Captain Shears."

"We need to get you inside the house to safety. I don't understand how they were able to sneak on the property, but it is not a good sign they are here."

"I am not going inside. You must help me find the lady Thorn wandered away with. I think she knows Charles's whereabouts."

"What makes you think that?"

"She is wearing Mother's necklace. Charles never goes anywhere without her necklace. Who do you think she is, Zane? How is she connected to Charles?"

Zane released Ivy, walked away from her, and ran his hand through his hair in frustration. He needed to confess his sins to Ivy. His friendship lay in the balance. He could not lie to her anymore. It would put her in more harm, but this needed to end tonight. It became increasingly dangerous. He would not risk her life anymore. The next time she wouldn't be safe, and Shears would grab her. He couldn't live with himself if he didn't put a stop to this madness.

Ivy watched Zane pace back and forth along the garden path. He seemed deep in thought as he weighed something heavy on his mind. Also, his behavior toward her changed dramatically. He no longer acted like the fun-loving friend, but more of a man who desired her. In all their years as friends, he never crossed the line as he had today. She sensed his desire earlier today, and again moments ago as he comforted her. Ivy didn't want to lose his friendship, but she needed to find out what troubled him into acting in this desperate behavior.

"What is the matter, Zane?"

Zane saw the concern on Ivy's face. Even through all her troubles and despair she still bestowed her friendship upon him. He hoped he would not lose it when he told her the truth.

"The lady you search for is Raina LeClair, and she holds information on the whereabouts of Charles."

"Raina LeClair. Is she the RL on the white linen from Thorn's room?"

"Yes."

"Does Thorn know her?"

"Yes, but I don't know how. He told me she is a part of his past."

"Is Charles in danger with this woman?

"At one time, I would have said yes."

"What does that mean?"

"She is working with Shears. But as she took care of your brother, I think her feelings changed. She has come to care for Charles very much."

"How do you know this?"

"It is a long story, Ivy. But the short of it is, I am just as much involved with Shears as Raina is."

Ivy stared at him in shock.

"Why?"

"Why what, Ivy?"

"Why on everything. Why Shears? Why Raina? Why Charles?"

"Shears has information I need. I have worked with him to gain his trust. Along the way, Raina was introduced into his plans. She began to change after she captured Charles. She found him along the side of the road and took him to her cottage. Raina wanted to seek her revenge against your family, so she held him hostage."

"What did my family ever do to her?"

"It was not your family, but who your family was connected to."

"Thorn?"

"Yes."

"What information would Shears have for you to betray your country? Are you a double agent?"

"I cannot answer those questions, Ivy. But I believe you know the true answers to them if you look deep enough into your heart."

"Do you know where Charles is right now?"

"Yes."

"Take me to him now, and we discuss this later. I am disappointed with you for keeping Charles's whereabouts from us."

"I hope one day you will be able to forgive me for all of this—and for what is to come."

Chapter Twenty-Seven

ZANE LED IVY TO the stables and saddled Mercury for them to ride. He lifted her in front of him, and they rode off. Ivy noticed Zane headed toward the cliffs. She wanted to tell him Thorn already searched the caves, but she stayed silent because obviously he knew more of Charles's whereabouts than she did.

As Ivy and Zane made the journey to the cliffs, a fog settled low. Zane led the horse along a path to the beach. Mercury was hesitant on their direction but allowed Zane to guide her along. He led the horse to a nearby tree, jumped down, and tied the horse to it. When he reached to pull Ivy off the horse, someone suddenly grabbed him from behind. Two men dragged Zane back and held him against his will.

"We will take it from here, Maxwell. Thank you for your assistance."

"Do not lay a hand on her, Shears. She is not part of the deal."

"Well, she is now. Take her to the ship and do not let her out of your sight this time," Shears ordered his men.

Ivy screamed as Shears's men pulled her off the horse and carried her to his ship. She struggled in their arms, lashing out any way she could. She screamed louder, hoping somebody would come to her rescue. The town was a half mile off the shore, so she hoped her screams would carry.

She managed to get one of her arms free, lashing out with a slap at the pirate and scratching her nails down his face. He dropped her at the attack, but the other pirate kept hauling her across the beach. Ivy dug her feet into the sand, trying to slow down her attacker. As Ivy's dress dragged along the water's edge, it made her heavier to carry, which made her unable to be carried very far.

"You men are worthless. How can you not handle one mere girl?" Shears shouted angrily at his crew.

He approached them and ripped the wet skirt from her dress. He picked up Ivy and threw her over his shoulder. She felt a sense of déjà vu. With panic overcoming her, Ivy fought her captor. She did not want this to play out into the same scene again. The captain only tightened his hold as he continued to the boat that would row them to his ship. Ivy needed saved before they reached the water's edge.

"Load Maxwell on the ship and continue to empty the cave. We need to leave before Thornhill realizes he is missing something." Shears laughed at his own joke.

The rest of his crew laughed along with him.

"You're a little too late for that. You will not be leaving anywhere tonight. Put her down, now."

Ivy heard Thorn but could not see him. Obviously, Shears did not know where he was because he turned them around in circles searching for him.

"Show yourself, Thornhill. You are outnumbered. My men have this beach surrounded."

Thorn laughed. "That is what you think. I will not repeat myself. I said to put her down. Now."

Shears set her down and pulled her in front of him as a shield. He slid an arm around her waist to keep her a prisoner against his body. Then with his other hand he pulled his knife from his waistband and slid it across her throat.

"Oh, I have put her down, Thornhill, but I will not release her now or anytime soon. I won't say it again. Show yourself or I will cut the little lady." He ran the blade across her cheek. "We would not want to mar this beautiful skin, would we, Captain?"

Thorn emerged from the trees. He was not alone. The mystery lady from the ball stood next to him. Thorn pulled her along after him. She struggled under his hold, but Thorn was determined she would stay with him. He had not yet decided which side she was on. She started on Shears side but after their conversation in the garden; he thinks she changed sides because of her feelings for Charles. But this was war and you couldn't trust anyone unless they held your heart in their hands.

"Maybe we can make a trade?" Thorn asked Shears.

Shears laughed. "You can keep that one; she is a traitor just like her father was."

"How do you know my father?" the young lady shouted.

"Who do you think had your father killed, mademoiselle? It was my crew who attacked Thornhill's ship. Your father double-crossed me on my arms deal. He developed a conscience after your mother and brother were killed. He didn't want his dealings to kill you too, so he made a deal with the captain there."

"But my mother and brother died in a carriage accident."

"Yes, I know," Shears said with a deadly smile.

"You animal. I am going to make sure you die."

The girl struggled out of Thorn's arms, advancing on Shears with her knife pulled out. Thorn managed to drag her back and grab the knife out of her hand.

"What do you want, Shears? Name your terms and I will meet them if you release Ivy."

"What, your precious Hedera?"

"Release her!" Thorn shouted.

"She does not know, does she? How quaint. Could never understand the name of your ship until I came across this delicious package. You chased me for years and ruined many deals for me. I tried for years to find your Achilles heel, until I ran across this quiet, sleepy little village. What a surprise when it came to my attention this was where you were from. Then when I discovered your Hedera was from there too, I realized I must have her for my own."

"Why would you want Thorn's ship for your own?" Ivy asked in confusion.

Shears laughed at her innocence.

"Not his ship, love. You."

"I don't understand."

"Do you want to tell her, Captain, or shall I? Oh, let me. I do love a good tale. Hedera stands for Ivy. He named his ship after you. It is such a romantic story. He must have loved you all along. But have you loved him too? Or do you love young Maxwell over there? Oh well, either way this tale will have a tragic ending. When I am done with you, neither one of them will want to touch you."

"If you lay one hand on her, I will hunt you down and kill you with my bare hands," Maxwell threatened as he struggled to get free.

"Oh, I adore a love triangle. Her charms must be delicious to have two gentlemen fighting for her honor. But the question is, who does Lady Ivy love? Does she love the captain who held a tender for her all these years? Or does she love the best friend she trusted who betrayed her trust and her country. Maxwell, you hold no bargaining power to make threats against me."

"It is not a threat, Shears."

"Well, I am not scared. It will be hard for you to harm me while they hang you for treason. Shall we tell your friends here of your involvement with my little terror plot I have organized on these English shores?"

"There is nothing to tell they probably have not already guessed," Maxwell replied.

"Yes, I can see that, but don't you think they want to hear the tiny little details on how you came to me to make this happen? If not for your involvement in the first place, we would not be here on these shores."

"Let him talk, Maxwell. I am curious of your involvement. I want to hear how you have placed Ivy's life in danger by bringing this scum into our lives. Then, I will take great pleasure in killing you after I kill him," Thorn said, nodding his head at Shears.

"No!" Ivy screamed at the threat to Zane. She couldn't let Thorn hurt him. Ivy had an idea why Zane involved himself with Shears, but she didn't want to blow Zane's cover. She would explain it to Thorn after they got free. Ivy tried to distract Shears to free herself from his grasp when she spotted Tommy out of the corner of her eye. He was coming to her rescue again. She saw he held a small pistol in his hand. His hands shook from fear, but he kept moving forward to help her.

"Let her go," the young voice rang out as he pointed the gun into Shears's back.

The captain turned at Tommy's voice, and Ivy relaxed her body into a faint, causing Shears to loosen his grip on her. Ivy broke free and ran from Shears. Thorn moved forward and pushed Ivy away from the captain's reach. Shears slapped Tommy across the face, sending him flying backward on the sand. The men who held Maxwell captive became distracted as they watched their captain attack the young cabin boy. Maxwell caught them unaware, throwing punches to set himself free. He knocked them out by striking them repeatedly across the face.

Meanwhile, Thorn advanced on Shears, pulling out his sword. The captain yanked out his sword, and they danced around each other. Each waited for the right moment and angle to strike one another. Their swords clashed against each other. They advanced and retreated, and their movements became quicker with each angry sweep of their arms, imposing danger onto one another.

Ivy ran toward Tommy and scooped him into her arms, carrying him to the safety of the trees. She owed the young boy her life once again. She would protect him and make sure no harm came to him. Thorn and she would make sure he had a place in their home. Ivy held the young boy, soothing him as Thorn defended her honor.

Thorn saw out of the corner of his eye that Ivy had gotten the young boy and herself to safety. He fought with all the anger and fear built inside him. His anger multiplied with each slash of his sword. He noticed Shears grew tired. He may play the part of a pirate, but he couldn't play the game as well. Thorn backed him against the wall outside the cave. With a quick jab of his sword, he knocked the sword from Shears's hand. He raised his sword to the captain's neck and held it there.

"It would be my greatest pleasure to end this now, but the King and England will take great pleasure in watching you hang. For now, I will take my pleasure as I hand you over to them," Thorn said as he slightly nicked his sword across the captain's neck, drawing blood.

Thorn raised his hand, giving the signal for Sammy and his crew to come out of hiding. Thorn's crew drifted from the shadows and gathered Shears's men. He turned Shears around and tied his hands behind his back and knocked him hard behind the knees to drop him to the ground.

"Grab the lanterns and search the caves. They hid Mallory inside one of them. Hurry. His life is in grave danger, and he must receive medical attention immediately," Thorn ordered.

Sammy lit a torch and entered the cave. Soon, he hollered that he'd found Charles, and Thorn rushed into the cave to rescue him. He carried him out and brought him over to lie beside Ivy. Thorn reached to cup Ivy's cheek.

"He is alive, my love."

With tears sliding slowly from her eyes, she turned her head and placed a soft kiss in his palm.

"Thank you, my love."

She feathered her shaking fingers through Charles's hair, tracing the bruises that covered his face. He moaned at her touch, whispering a name that wasn't hers.

"Raina?"

"No, Charles. It's Ivy. You are safe now."

He drifted back to unconscious. Ivy searched the darkness, softly lit by the torches, for Raina. The lady had disappeared.

"Thorn, where did she go?"

Thorn stood to look around for Raina. She was nowhere to be seen. In all the distraction, she disappeared into the foggy night. They would find her later, but she was the least of his concerns at the moment. For she wasn't the only one attempting to disappear. Thorn turned in a circle as he looked for Maxwell. He lost sight of him as he saw to Mallory's rescue.

He glanced to where he left Shears and saw he was gone too. Thorn took off to where he'd last left Shears and noticed Maxwell aiding Shears in his getaway. They climbed into a boat farther up the beach. Thorn ran, trying to reach them before they pushed off from the shore. Once they hit the water, he had no way to get to them. There were no other boats around. Thorn saw the oars hit the water and was about to jump into the sea. He could swim to the boat and stop them. Before he reached the water, a shot rang out, the bullet flying past his ear.

"Stop, Thorn. I missed you on purpose, but if you continue to pursue us, the next shot will hit its mark. I will not do that to Ivy if I do not have to. If you love her, you will stop there," Maxwell yelled.

Thorn came skidding to a halt. He knew Maxwell could have shot him spot on if he wanted to. He was an excellent marksman. Thorn also realized something desperate pushed Maxwell into collaboration with Shears. When men were desperate, they did desperate things. He lifted his hands and backed away from the water.

"You won't get far, Maxwell. Come back, and we can help you. Mallory and I will make sure you don't hang. You do not have to sink any lower with that scum."

Maxwell laughed. "That is where you are wrong, my friend. Give Ivy my love and treat her like the precious gem she is. If you don't, I will return and see that I do."

Shears and Maxwell continued rowing to the ship. Thorn was unable to put a stop to them. He would have to alert the proper authorities, but for now, Charles needed immediate medical attention. Everything else could wait. He instructed Sammy to gather the men Shears abandoned, empty the cave of weapons, and bring them to Thornhill. Once they were there, he would send for the King's men to arrest them for treason and destroy the weapons.

Thorn walked to Ivy, lifted her into his arms, and climbed onto Mercury's back. His men loaded Charles and the young cabin boy onto the bed of a wagon Shears's men had used to transport the weapons. They slowly made their return to Thornhill.

As they approached the house Thorn noticed the ball was over. He realized a big scandal would spread through the gossip mill. Their early departure from their betrothal ball would be the gossip story of the season. It would quiet down again as soon as he walked Ivy in front of the preacher and spoke their vows. He trusted his parents to have kept some of the rumors at bay. The one shining light of the evening was finding Charles and bringing him home.

He held onto Ivy tightly, placing soft kisses on her head as they rode back. He never felt fear like he did when Shears held a knife to her throat. Her body relaxed into his from sheer exhaustion as she melted against him. He wanted to shower her with kisses, hold on to her, and never let her go. He was thankful she came out of this ordeal with no harm done to her. They didn't speak a word as they held each other close.

When they arrived home, their parents came rushing out to them. Katherine wrapped Ivy in a quilt. She yelled orders to the staff, directing them where to take Charles and the young boy they brought home. George and Hamilton went to the wagon and helped the footmen carry Charles.

They carried him inside, taking him to the family wing into a bedroom prepared for him.

"Take her to her room, Marcus. Mabel waits there for her with a bath. The doctor is already here and will see to Charles. There is nothing for Ivy to do until the doctor finishes with him. Make sure she gets a little rest. Then we will discuss the outcome of tonight's adventure," Katherine ordered him. She gave him a kiss on the cheek. "I am so glad you children are all right, my son. I love you."

"I love you, Mother." Marcus returned her kiss on the cheek.

He lifted Ivy into his arms and carried her upstairs to her room. Mabel was there to take care of her. He lowered her to her feet and brushed a kiss across her forehead. He wanted to stay with her but knew he couldn't.

"Take a bath, my love. I will return to you later," he whispered in her ear. He took her lips in a soft gentle kiss.

As he walked to the door to leave, he sensed her watching him. As he turned, he stared as Mabel urged her over to the bath. She smiled at him in her shy, sweet way that always touched his heart. He smiled back at her with all his love.

He continued to his own bedroom to change his clothes. When he entered his room, he went to his desk and slid open the secret door in his drawer. Thorn reached into his pocket and pulled out the same stone he returned to Maxwell earlier in the evening. In all the commotion, the stone must have slipped out of Maxwell's pocket. He slid the stone into the hiding place and closed the drawer. He smiled to himself as he changed his clothes, secure in the knowledge Maxwell would return to him one day after all. When he did, Thorn would be ready for him.

Chapter Twenty-Eight

THORN CHANGED INTO A fresh pair of clothes and headed toward Charles's room. The doctor finished examining him and professed him to be badly injured, but he wasn't in any grave danger. Whoever took care of him did an excellent job, and they had saved his life. He was on the mend and would make a full recovery. The doctor gave him a small dose of laudanum for his pain. He told Thorn that Charles was upset and wanted to look for somebody named Raina. Charles's father managed to quiet him down with a promise they would search for her. Thorn left the nurse to tend to Charles for the night.

As he walked along the hallway, he noticed the house had quieted itself. He passed Mabel in the hallway with a report that Ivy had fallen asleep on the bed in sheer exhaustion. Thorn sent Mabel back to bed and ordered her to sleep in tomorrow. He waited until Mabel took the stairs to the servants' quarters before he snuck into Ivy's room.

When he entered Ivy's bedroom, he noticed Mabel left the windows open. The breeze blew the curtains in a slow dance against the windows. He looked over and saw Ivy asleep on top of her bedding with a light blanket draped across her body. Thorn stood at the windows as he let the soft breeze calm his soul as he gazed at the woman he loved. He almost lost her tonight before he could make her his wife. What a fool he had been all these years.

When he did finally come to his senses, it put her in grave danger and almost made him lose her.

Thorn moved across the space of the bedroom and knelt at her side of the bed. He drew her hand into his as he lifted it to his lips, softly kissing her fingers.

"I promise from this day forth you will always know of my love for you. I will protect you for the rest of our lives together," he whispered.

Ivy stirred at his words, slowly opening her eyes. She blinked the sleep from her eyes.

"Marcus?" she whispered.

"My sweet Ivy," he whispered back before he drew her into his arms and kissed her with the emotion of his love for her. He poured his heart and soul into her body with his kisses. Marcus slid onto the bed, drawing her body alongside his. His hands roamed over her body, greedily wanting to touch every silken inch of her.

Ivy kissed him back with all her passion and love for him. Her hands slid underneath his shirt, drawing it over his head. Her fingers fumbled as they tried to unbutton his trousers, and Marcus reached to help her. After he removed his hands, Ivy began to undress him again. She slid his trousers off his legs, then her hands slid back up. Her hands moved along his thighs, and she hesitated when she reached his hardness. She stared into Marcus's eyes and saw his desire and need for her touch. He nodded his head at her touch. She slid her fingers softly over him as his heat scorched her fingers. Ivy wanted to burn from him as she slid her hand around him, feeling him throb against her fingertips. She watched him close his eyes in agony at her touch. She started to withdraw, as she thought she hurt him, but he shook his head no and held her hand around him. Ivy tightened her fingers as she let him guide her hand on how to please him.

He withdrew his hand as she stroked him to a fever pitch. He moaned as her fingers slid up and down, the flame growing hotter at every stroke of her hand. She realized the power her touch held over him, and it enflamed her soul. His flame flowed into her body, bringing her into the fire with him. For every stroke of her hand was the stroke of his hand on her body. He stripped her of her nightgown and carried her body along with his. His hands caressed her breasts as his lips kissed her body hungrily. She felt the heat pooling between her thighs. Her body ached at the passion and grew hotter and hotter at every touch he trailed along her body.

They spoke no words, for they had none to speak that could describe the feelings they held for one another. They let their hands and mouths convey their feelings instead.

Marcus slid his fingers to her core and slid his finger inside her. Ivy arched her body at his touch, wanting more. He felt the heat of her at every stroke of his finger. His body wanted to be wrapped inside her before she exploded. He wanted to sink into the flames with her.

He pulled Ivy closer to his body and crashed his mouth upon hers. Marcus kissed her hungrily as his tongue stroked hers as he squeezed her to him. Their mouths drew their passion higher and higher as he slid her beneath him. He drew away as he stared into her eyes and saw the passion and love clouding her eyes. Marcus stared at her as he slid inside her heat slowly. He moved deep inside her as every flame licked him when he moved in deeper. He continued gazing into her eyes as they darkened with desire.

Ivy stared into Marcus's eyes as he slowly moved his body into hers. She raised her hips to bring his heat deeper inside her. Her fingers gripped his arms as their bodies built the fire higher. Marcus slid long, deep strokes in an out of her, leaving Ivy with wanting more. His love for her invaded her soul with every stroke, touch, and kiss. Ivy sensed his desperation at their lovemaking. She understood he was afraid he almost lost her tonight, but she needed to let him know they would be all right.

She reached to slide her fingers through his hair, brushing it back from his face, and rose to softly kiss him on his lips. Her lips soothed his tortured soul and let him know she was safe in his arms. She continued kissing him softly as her fingers stroked his body, calming him. She moved her hips along with his, slowly drawing out every flame. Their bodies became one, and as their souls met, they fell off their cliff into the cool blue sea they both loved. As their bodies floated on the clear water, they clung to each other, drifting to sleep in each other's arms.

Thorn awoke early the next morning as the sun rose. He could hear the servants downstairs moving around as they started their day. He needed to rise and return to his own bedroom before anybody caught him in Ivy's room. As he gazed at the woman in his arms, he realized that while they found Charles, Ivy was still in danger from Shears. He placed a kiss on top of her head as he slid out from underneath her. He smiled, watching her sleep as he got dressed. Thorn needed to talk to Charles before everybody else woke and questioned him.

Chapter Twenty-Nine

HE LEFT IVY AND strolled to Charles's room. Thorn dismissed the nurse, ordering her to eat breakfast and that he would sit with the patient until she returned. He stretched out on the chair as he waited for Charles to awaken. He closed his eyes, only to open them again when he heard Charles's scratchy voice.

"Is she gone yet?"

Thorn laughed. Charles always hated to be told what to do and hated lying around even more. Thorn reached for the pitcher of water and poured Charles a glass. He tried bringing it to Charles lips to drink to only have Charles reach and grab it out of his hand. Charles gulped it and motioned for Thorn to refill his glass. He drank the next glass more slowly, then leaned back and closed his eyes.

There was complete silence in the room, and Thorn listened to Charles' breathing deepen. He thought he fell back to sleep, only to be questioned by him again.

"Are the rumors true? Did you ruin my sister, Thornhill?"

"Now, where would you hear those kinds of rumors?" Thorn questioned back.

"Well, from the nurse and the maid gossiping when they thought I was sleeping. One heard how both of you ran away together from a London ball to Gretna Green and the other heard Ivy stowed away on your ship. Either way, she came back ruined, and now you two must get married. But of course, they both made it seem much more romantic in their stories," Mallory said with sarcasm.

"I love her, Charles."

"And she loves you. But did you have to ruin her, Marcus? She deserved so much more. She has waited for you for years."

"I know, and I wanted to give her all that. I didn't set out to ruin her. If it wasn't for me rescuing her, she would be ruined in a way in which none of us could fix."

Charles closed his eyes and realized Thorn was correct. He just didn't have to like it. They had been best friends all their lives, but Ivy was his sister. Her happiness came first. Charles opened his eyes again and regarded his best friend. He could tell Thorn wanted his approval of the match but was too proud to ask for it. He reached out his hand for Thorn to shake.

"Make her happy every day of her life and love her like she deserves to be loved."

"I promise, my friend." Thorn shook Charles's hand.

"What will you do now?" Thorn asked Charles.

"I'm going after all of them."

"When?"

"After the wedding. I cannot let their trail grow cold. It will be long enough for me to heal."

"Charles, I understand your need to go after Maxwell and Shears, but you need more time to heal. Let me send my men to track them. I will have Sammy and Jake look for them, and they will keep us informed of their whereabouts."

"I appreciate the offer, but I need to do this myself. The information I have will get me in and out of places faster if I am alone. You need to keep Ivy safe and out of harm's way the best you can."

"I will try. She will not like you following after them. She thinks Maxwell isn't a danger to any of us. He shot at me last night to warn me off. Do you know why he's working with Shears?"

"No, but it will be one question I will get an answer for."

Thorn reached into his pocket and withdrew the handkerchief, throwing it over to Charles. It landed on top of the covers. He watched as Charles traced the initials RL over and over.

"Are you going after her too?"

"Yes."

"Do you think that is wise?"

"I don't know."

"I wouldn't trust her, Charles. She is involved with Maxwell and Shears."

"There are many things you do not understand about her."

"I know she is not to be trusted, and she is out for revenge."

"Not toward me, she isn't."

Thorn realized he wouldn't get through to him and decided to find out how Charles felt about Raina. He noticed how she cared for Charles and wondered if Charles felt the same.

"Do you care for the girl?"

"I have feelings for her, and I must understand what they are and if she returns them. I will not walk away like you did with Ivy."

Thorn nodded his head, Charles was right. He was the fool seven years ago. His friend held more nerve than he ever did. He would not stand in his way, but he would caution him to be careful.

"Just be careful, my friend, and come back to us safely. Now get some more rest before the rest of the family wants to visit with you. You won't get any after Ivy awakens."

"Thank you for everything, Thorn."

"That is what friends are for."

Chapter Thirty

WHEN IVY AWOKE NEXT, it was to find herself alone in bed. She looked around for Marcus, but her room was empty. She lay back on the bed, smoothing the sheet beside her, and wondered if it was all a dream. When she glanced over on the other pillow, she noticed the rose. A piece of ivy was wound through the thorns. She lifted the rose and smiled to herself. It wasn't a dream, Marcus had made soul-searching love with her last night.

Ivy then remembered everything from the night before. They'd rescued Charles. She needed to talk with him, as they still had much to learn. But for now, she only wanted to see if he was safe.

She rang for Mabel to help her dress. Mabel brought in tea and toast with instructions from Thorn to eat before she joined them. They would wait for her in Charles's room. She listened to Mabel jabber about how the ton wondered where they ran off to. There were rumors already floating around they had snuck away to Gretna Green to elope. Ivy listened to Mabel smiling at everything the young girl gossiped about. She realized none of it mattered. All that mattered was that they'd found Charles safe and that she would be wed to Thorn soon.

Ivy finished dressing and ran down the hallway to Charles's bedroom. She rushed inside his room and saw him sitting in bed eating breakfast. She ran and jumped on the bed, hugging him.

"Oh, Charles, you had us so worried. I am so glad you are safe."

Everybody laughed at Ivy's greeting, even Charles. He winced at her enthusiasm. He was still sore around the ribs. Thorn noticed his discomfort and pulled Ivy away.

"Easy love, he is still a bit sore."

"I am sorry, Charles. I'm just so happy we've found you." Ivy sat back on the bed, reaching for his hand. "You must tell us everything."

Charles explained to the family how he worked with the Crown to stop the treason plot. He laid out Shears's involvement with the French government and their plans to bring the war onto English soil. He infiltrated their organization to learn the ins and outs of their plans. Charles was close to learning when it would all take place when they sabotaged him outside the Margate Inn and kidnapped Ivy.

His memory was unclear after that. He said he drifted in and out of conscious since he was badly beaten. Charles could only recall bits and pieces of his time away. He remembered a young lady named Raina who took care of him. He realized she was out for revenge at first, while she held him captive in her cabin. Over time, they came to care for one another, and she softened toward him. He explained how she feared Shears and that was the reason why she ran away.

"But how does Maxwell play into all of this?" Thorn asked.

"It is complicated, most of what I am not at liberty to say. It is top government information. But from where it stands, if you say he left with Shears on his own free will instead of keeping him captured, he will be a wanted man. I worked alongside him on this assignment, but all along I had a sense he had his own agenda. I only hope he finds what he seeks before it gets him killed."

The room stayed quiet as everybody processed their own thoughts on Maxwell's level of guilt. Ivy felt in her heart whatever he was after was not done for treason but for what he held in his own heart. She hoped he stayed safe and solved his problems to come home again.

"I am grateful to you Thorn, my friend, for rescuing Ivy. We all know it was not the first time and certainly will not be the last. I hope you are prepared for a long life of it," Charles teased.

Thorn laughed and pulled Ivy up into his arms for a hug.

"It is something I very much look forward to. You better get healed enough to walk. We have a wedding in a week. I need my best man to stand up with me."

"I would be honored, Thorn," Charles replied.

"Well then, let us leave so you can rest. Ivy, you come with me. We have our final preparations for the wedding. You men can take care of the cargo that arrived overnight in the stable yard and dispense with it accordingly," Katherine directed.

They left Charles to rest. As their parents walked downstairs, Thorn tugged Ivy into a tiny alcove for a kiss.

"One more week, my love, and you will be all mine," Thorn said.

"Finally, Thorn. I was beginning to wonder if you were ever going to come to your senses," Ivy teased.

"Imp." Thorn kissed Ivy thoroughly for her teasing, leaving her light-headed as he spun her away from him.

Ivy laughed as Thorn ran down the stairs after their fathers. She smiled to herself as she watched him hurry after them. She would join Katherine soon, but she needed to talk with Charles a little more. Ivy sensed something bothered him, and she wanted to help if she could. Ivy returned to his room and slid the door open quietly, not wanting to wake him if he had fallen asleep. But Charles wasn't lying in bed. He stood at the window, looking at something in his hands.

"Charles, are you all right? You seem lost."

Charles's head rose at the sound of Ivy's voice. He watched his sister walk into the room and over to his side. Ivy had always been his confidant. It bothered him when he could not tell her about his work for the Crown. If he had, perhaps she wouldn't have been so curious and followed him everywhere. It was her curiosity that landed them in grave danger. He should have trusted her with his secret. But then, if all of this had not happened, he would never have met Raina.

"I guess I am a little. I feel as if I have lost a part of my soul that I don't know if I will ever get back."

"You will recover fully, Charles," Ivy replied. She misunderstood him.

He smoothed the piece of linen out Thorn returned to him earlier. Thorn explained how he found the clue in their secret cave. Charles told him he left it there for him to discover to let him know he was alive. He slid his fingers over the initials RL, hoping for any kind of connection with her.

Ivy saw what Charles held in his possession—the handkerchief from Thorn's room. She wondered how Charles had it. The last time she had seen it was when Zane took it.

"Where did you get that, Charles?"

"Thorn returned it to me. It belongs to Raina."

"Why would he give it to you? Doesn't it belong to somebody he cared about, a memento?"

"Ivy, the only woman Thorn cares about or has ever cared about is you, silly goose."

"But he kept it hidden in his room among his personal items."

"You are letting your imagination get away with you again," Charles teased.

Ivy curled up in the oversized chair next to his bed. She patted the bed for him to lie back down. Charles moved to the bed slowly and slid under the covers. He closed his eyes, weary from the short journey.

"Tell me the story behind it," Ivy urged.

"This belongs to Raina LeClair. She is the young lady from the beach who used to be involved with Shears. When she decided I was not a threat, she saw how wrong she was in her revenge, and we moved locations where Shears couldn't find us. That was when I took her to the cave. While we hid at the cave waiting for Maxwell to come take us to a more secure location he found, my wounds opened, and I bled badly. Raina used her handkerchief to stop the bleeding. I left it there because I knew Thorn would search the cave. I wanted him to understand I was well."

"Zane knew all along where you were. Why would he lie to me?" Ivy asked, hurt and confused.

"Because I told him not to tell anybody about my whereabouts. Maxwell told me how Shears and his men waited to capture you again. I didn't want to risk you coming after me. We decided he would act his carefree self and learn any new information from Thorn."

Ivy sat quiet for a while. It frustrated her that all the men in her life wanted to shelter her. She understood they did it out of love, but it hurt when Zane thought he couldn't confide in her. He was obviously troubled over something. She wished she could help him, but she couldn't.

"Why did you look so lost when I came in?"

"I am worried about her, Ivy. I don't know where she has gone, and I am too weak to find her. Thorn has men searching for her, but they won't find her. She knows how to live underground."

"You care for her, don't you?"

Charles looked at Ivy and nodded. He did not quite understand the depth of his emotions, as they were all new to him, but he realized he cared for her.

"You gave her Mother's necklace."

"Yes, it was to be a sign for you to know I was alive."

"When I tried to confront her, she ran."

"Something or somebody must have spooked her."

"Why do you want to look for her? You need time to heal. Also, you still need to bring Shears to a halt."

"She has nobody, Ivy. I have developed emotions for her I do not understand. What I must do is find her and keep her safe. She is a good person and has been through many horrible ordeals in her life."

Ivy reached over and squeezed her brother's hand. Her brother had the kindest heart. If Charles saw good in Raina, then there was good in her. She would support her brother and help him in any way she could.

"Well then, we must get you feeling better, so you can find her. If you like her, then I will too." Ivy leaned over and brushed a kiss across his cheek.

"Thank you for understanding."

Ivy squeezed his hand in reply.

"I am finally glad to see you have brought our boy to his knees. You took long enough."

Ivy smiled, "I love him so much, Charles. He has made me the happiest girl in the world."

"I know he has, and you have made him just as happy. I wish you two the very best."

"Get some rest. We have a wedding you need to attend soon," Ivy ordered as she left the room.

~~~~~~~

Thorn walked toward the stable where George and Hamilton directed the men on the destructions of the weapons. The authorities arrived, and they loaded Shears's men onto the wagons and into custody. They would take them to Newgate Prison in London. There would be no trial for these men because they were caught committing acts of treason against the Crown. They would hang for their crimes. Since everything seemed to be taken care of, Thorn wandered further into the stables as he looked for young Tommy. He found him in a stall, playing with the newborn kittens.

"You can have one for your own," Thorn offered as he knelt to pet the kittens.

"But I don't have anywhere to keep one, sir?"

"Well that is why I am here. I was wondering if you would like to stay with Ivy and me."

"Really?" Tommy asked.

"Yes, really," Thorn chuckled.

"I would love to work for you."

"Not work, Tommy. Live with us as our son. I owe you a huge debt of gratitude. You have saved my lady's life twice now."

Tommy lowered his head as Thorn praised him, embarrassed by the compliments.

"It would be my honor, sir."

"I only ask one thing for now. We must keep this a secret from Lady Ivy. I think this would make a very nice wedding present. Don't you agree?"

Tommy jumped in excitement and hugged Thorn. He backed away quickly and bent over to lift a kitten.

"I will keep our secret."

Thorn patted Tommy on the shoulders as he exited the stall. He smiled as he thought of Ivy's reaction to this news.

Chapter Thirty-One

THE MORNING OF THEIR wedding arrived. It was a beautiful summer day full of sunshine and love in the air. The church was filled with Katherine's beloved roses. Thorn waited for Ivy at the altar of Thornhill Church. They packed the pews with the well-wishers and gossipers who wanted to catch a glimpse of the lovely couple. He waited with calm as Ivy appeared in the doorway. She took his breath away with her loveliness. She floated down the aisle on George's arm, smiling all the way. Her smile was filled with confidence of the love they shared, and it took his breath away.

They joined hands at the altar and spoke their vows in front of their loved ones. After the ceremony, their family and friends wished them well. Ivy glimpsed Tommy standing with their family, dressed as a proper young gentleman. He winked at her as she walked down the aisle on Marcus's arm.

Ivy stopped and knelt to his height.

"Well, don't you look like a proper gent," Ivy teased.

Tommy bowed before her.

"Can we tell her the good news, sir?" Tommy looked at Thorn as he loudly whispered his request.

"I think she may receive her wedding present now," Thorn whispered back.

"What is all this secrecy?" Ivy joined their whispering.

Thorn rested his hand on Tommy's shoulder, gently squeezing. "I have asked young Thomas here if he would like to be our son, and he has agreed."

Ivy brought her hand to her mouth and let out a gasp. Tears came to her eyes as she looked at Marcus in surprise. When he nodded his head to her unasked question, she wrapped her arms around Tommy and hugged him.

"This is the best wedding present I could have ever received," she told Tommy, kissing him on the cheek.

Tommy blushed but returned Ivy's hug. He never felt the arms of a mother before, and realized he would enjoy Lady Ivy's hugs.

Ivy rose and kissed Thorn on the cheek. She laced her fingers with his, then held her other hand out for Tommy to hold as they walked out of the church as a family.

Katherine guided the guests back to the house for the breakfast reception. Tommy returned to the house with his new grandparents. Thorn had plans of his own before they made their appearance as husband and wife. As he loaded Ivy into the carriage, he whispered his plan to Sammy. Sammy took them on a detour, dropping them off at the back of the rose garden.

"Why are we stopping here, Marcus?"

"I have a surprise for you, my dear wife."

"I love the sound of that."

"And I love saying it, my dear wife."

Ivy smiled at him as he guided her to the same exact spot they kissed all those years ago. Marcus gathered her hands in his and leaned over to kiss her. He kissed her as he had kissed her for their first time. The kiss started off slow and gentle with passion overtaking it as it had long ago.

"I was a fool all those years ago, Ivy. I will continue to make many foolish mistakes in our years to come, but I will never run from our love again. I love you, my sweet Ivy."

"I love you, Marcus Thornhill. With all my heart. I loved you then as a girl, but I will love you for the rest of our days as your wife. We will make mistakes together, but our love will correct them."

"I have a present for you."

"Oh, but I have nothing for you."

"Your love is the only present I need and want. I brought you here because this place holds a special meaning in both of our hearts. It is here I wish to speak to you of my love."

Marcus guided Ivy to the bench next to the waterfall and sat beside her. He held onto her hands as he smiled into her eyes. When he spoke the words, Ivy was so overcome by his love for her, she could only listen.

<u>Ivy My Love</u>

Your love is like a vine

Forever clinging to my heart.

It tangles in between my jagged thorns.

I try to break apart

To free myself from your love,

But you have grown so heavy in my thoughts.

I will let you go for now

For you need to grow wild and free,

But I will return to you with my love,

And our love will cling forever between the ivy and the

thorns.

"I return to you with my love, and I pledge my promise to you to never break apart from our love again."

Tears of happiness slid from Ivy's eyes as she smiled at him. Her love finally came home to her. Their first kiss, to the empty years without him, had led them to this moment of true joy. Ivy would not have it had any other way. It was what made their love unbreakable.

Ivy snuggled into Thorn on the bench and whispered her words of love to him, stealing kisses in between, as Thorn held her, content in their love.

It was there Katherine found them holding hands, kissing, and laughing like two young children in love. She smiled her happiness at the love they finally found in each other. As she glanced to the sky, she smiled at her friend and winked. She returned to the reception as she left them to their happiness.

Epilogue

IVY BACKED OUT OF the room quietly, closing the door behind her; she didn't want to awaken Tommy. Thorn exhausted him on his first day in London with sightseeing. It was hard to calm him from all his excitement. He told her they rode through Hyde Park and visited the Tower Bridge. Tommy told Ivy that Thorn bought him an ice, and they watched the ships on the Thames as they crossed under the bridge. Ivy finally settled him to sleep with promises of more sightseeing tomorrow.

She smiled to herself at what a wonderful addition he made to their family as she slid her hand across her stomach. He would make a terrific older brother. She couldn't wait to tell Thorn her delightful news. That was why she stayed behind today, so she could visit the doctor. Ivy passed Sims, the butler of Hillston House on her way to Thorn's study.

"That will be all tonight Sims. The staff may have an early night." Ivy smiled sweetly at him.

He bowed as he said, "Thank you, Lady Ivy. I will inform the staff."

Ivy watched as Sims gathered the footmen and ushered them below stairs. She heard him tell the staff to finish for the night and to retire to their rooms. She smiled to herself at what they must think of her giving them permission to retire when it was still light outside. It was the only time she could get Thorn to herself with Tommy afoot. She was so excited to share this wonderful news with him.

She slid open the study door, locked it behind her, and leaned against the doors, holding onto the door handles. Ivy watched Thorn read a letter with a serious expression on his face. He still did not notice that Ivy had entered the room. Ivy moved across the room to stand in front of his mahogany desk and still he did not acknowledge her presence. She tilted her head to the side as she tried to recognize who had written him such a serious letter. Still unable to figure out who wrote the letter and unable to draw Thorn's attention, Ivy released a little cough.

Thorn looked in confusion at Ivy standing in front of his desk. When had she entered the room? He glanced past her and saw the study door closed and the house silent. When he looked at Ivy again, he read the curiosity in her eyes. He would have to show her the letter. It would upset her, but it was far better than her trying to find out any other way. When she tried to learn things her way, it only ended in more trouble.

"It is from Charles, my dear."

Ivy ran around the desk and tore the letter from Thorn's hand. He stared as she paced in front of the fireplace back and forth, reading the letter. He needed to keep her calm because of the news she wanted to share with him. She didn't go with them today because the doctor paid her a visit.

He smiled to himself that Ivy thought she could keep this kind of secret from him. There was no other person who understood her body like him. There were slight changes in the last month, and the carriage ride to London confirmed his suspicions. When she wasn't sleeping, she was getting sick, and they'd had to pull the carriage to the side of the road many times.

"He thinks he has found her but is watching her activities. He has not seen any sign of Zane or Shears in his search," Ivy told Thorn.

"I know, love."

"What is he waiting for? He told me he has feelings for her, so why doesn't he talk to her?"

"It is complicated. He may have feelings for her, but he does not trust her. She could still be connected with Shears, and it would only put Charles in danger if he played his hand too soon."

"I worry about him, Thorn."

Thorn reached his hand out for Ivy to come over to him. Ivy grabbed his hand and slid onto his lap. Thorn wrapped her in his arms holding her close. He ran his hand down through her hair, stroking it softly. She nestled in closer, feeling secure in his arms.

"I know you do. He is playing it safer this time around. He keeps in contact with us, so we know where he is. But the fact of the matter is that he still has a mission to complete."

"I know, but it will not stop me from worrying less."

They sat in silence, each other's thoughts about Charles scattered in different directions. Ivy hoped he found what he searched for in Raina and located Zane to talk some sense into him. She did not want him anywhere near Shears but understood he must be to complete his mission. Thorn had not shown Ivy the other part of the letter that he slid into the top drawer of his desk. He read that part of the letter first. Charles wrote them two different sets of letters. One for Thorn's eyes only and the other to share with Ivy. It was the first letter Thorn thought of now.

Shears was in the area but without Zane. Charles feared for Raina's safety but was unable to convince her of his help. He would write soon, after he discovered more on Shears's activities. Ivy's life would always be at risk as long as Shears was on the loose. His need to keep Ivy safe was more important now than ever. He slid his palm over her stomach, softly caressing it.

Ivy stared into Thorn's eyes as she felt his caress. He knew. He smiled at her and placed a gentle kiss on her lips.

"Do you have something to tell me, my love?"

"How do you know?"

"Ivy, my dear, I know everything there is to know about you. Am I correct in what I am thinking? Am I going to be a father?"

Ivy wrapped her arms around his neck pulling him down for a sweet kiss.

"Yes, my love. You will be a father in seven months' time. Are you happy?"

Thorn stood with Ivy in his arms and swung her around, kissing her with all his happiness.

"You have made me the happiest man on earth again."

"Thorn, please stop. You're making me dizzy," Ivy pleaded, feeling sick again.

Thorn noticed how pale Ivy was from his excitement, and he gently lowered her to the couch. He lay next to her, curving her body along his. He placed soft kisses across her brow and down to her lips.

"I am sorry, love."

Ivy cupped his cheek as she smiled at him. His enthusiasm made her secure in their love. He would make a wonderful father to their children. All her dreams came true because of him. It all started with a kiss in the rose garden. She hoped they had a girl so they could name her Rose.

Thorn returned Ivy's smile. She was so precious to him and the love of his life. To imagine he almost walked away from it all. He hoped they had a girl just like her mama. With long blonde hair, green eyes, and a curiosity for all things.

"Thorn?"

"Yes, my dear," he said as he bent to kiss her gently on the lips.

"I gave the staff the rest of the evening off."

Thorn threw back his head and laughed for the pure joy of it. His little minx.

"Well, we better take full advantage of this time, my dear," he said as he peeled her dress away from her body kissing her as he went along.

Ivy laughed with love. "I love you, Marcus Thornhill."

"And I love you, my sweet Ivy."

Look for Charles & Raina's story in *Rescued By the Spy*

"Thank you for reading Rescued By the Captain. Gaining exposure as an independent author relies mostly on word-of-mouth, so if you have the time and inclination, please consider leaving a short review wherever you can."

*Visit my website **www.lauraabarnes.com** to join my mailing list.*

Author Laura A. Barnes

International selling author Laura A. Barnes fell in love with writing in the second grade. After her first creative writing assignment, she knew what she wanted to become. Many years went by with Laura filling her head full of story ideas and some funny fish songs she wrote while fishing with her family. Thirty-seven years later, she made her dreams a reality. With her debut novel *Rescued By the Captain*, she has set out on the path she always dreamed about.

When not writing, Laura can be found devouring her favorite romance books. Laura is married to her own Prince Charming (who for some reason or another thinks the heroes in her books are about him) and they have three wonderful children and two sweet grandbabies. Besides her love of reading and writing, Laura loves to travel. With her passport stamped in England, Scotland, and Ireland; she hopes to add more countries to her list soon.

While Laura isn't very good on the social media front, she loves to hear from her readers. You can find her on the following platforms:

You can visit her at *www.lauraabarnes.com* to join her mailing list.

Website: **http://www.lauraabarnes.com**
Amazon: **https://amazon.com/author/lauraabarnes**
Goodreads: **https://www.goodreads.com/author/show/16332844.Laura_A_Barnes**
Facebook: **https://www.facebook.com/AuthorLauraA.Barnes/**
Instagram: **https://www.instagram.com/labarnesauthor/**
Twitter: **https://twitter.com/labarnesauthor**
BookBub: **https://www.bookbub.com/profile/laura-a-barnes**

Desire other books to read by Laura A. Barnes

Enjoy these other historical romances:

Matchmaking Madness Series:
How the Lady Charmed the Marquess

Tricking the Scoundrels Series:
Whom Shall I Kiss... An Earl, A Marquess, or A Duke?
Whom Shall I Marry... An Earl or A Duke?
I Shall Love the Earl
The Scoundrel's Wager
The Forgiven Scoundrel

Romancing the Spies Series:
Rescued By the Captain
Rescued By the Spy
Rescued By the Scot

Fiction
1

Made in the USA
Middletown, DE
14 November 2020